The Scarlet Pimpernel

Gift Classics available in Armada include

THE SCARLET PIMPERNEL

Baroness Orczy

Edited and abridged by
Doris Dickens

Illustrations by

James Mayhew

ARMADA

First published in this illustrated edition
in the U.K. in Armada in 1989

Armada is an imprint of
the Children's Division, part of
the Collins Publishing Group,
8 Grafton Street, London W1X 3LA

Printed and bound in Great Britain by
William Collins Sons & Co. Ltd, Glasgow

Contents

CHAPTER 1

Paris: September 1792

A surging, seething, murmuring crowd of beings that are human only in name, for to the eye and ear they seem nothing but savage creatures, full of vile passions, vengeance and hate. The hour, some little time before sunset, and the place, the West Barricade, Paris.

During the greater part of the day the guillotine had been kept busy at its ghastly work: all that France had boasted of in the past centuries, of ancient names, and blue blood, had paid the price of her desire for liberty and for fraternity. The slaughter had only ceased at this late hour of the day because there were other more interesting sights for the people to witness, a little while before the final closing of the barricades for the night.

And so the crowd rushed away from the Place de la Grève and made for the various barricades in order to watch this interesting and amusing sight.

It was to be seen every day, for those aristos were such

7

fools! They were traitors to the people of course, all of them, men, women, and children who happened to be descendants of the great men who, since the Crusades, had made the glory of France: her old nobility. Their ancestors had oppressed the people, had crushed them under the scarlet heels of their dainty buckled shoes, and now the people had become the rulers of France, and crushed their former masters – not beneath their heel, for they went shoeless mostly in these days – but beneath the knife of the guillotine.

And daily, hourly, this hideous instrument of torture claimed its many victims – old men, young women, tiny children, even until the day when it would finally demand the head of a king and of a beautiful young queen.

The victims tried to hide and tried to fly: that was just the fun of the whole thing. Every afternoon before the gates closed and the market carts went out in procession by the various barricades, some fool of an aristo tried to escape the clutches of the Committee of Public Safety. In various disguises, they tried to slip through the barriers which were so well guarded by citizen soldiers of the Republic. Men dressed as women, women dressed as men, children disguised in beggars' rags: there were all sorts: counts, marquises, even dukes, who were trying to escape to England or some other accursed foreign country – traitors all and enemies of the glorious Revolution.

But they were nearly always caught at the barricades. At the West Gate Sergeant Bibot especially had a wonderful nose for scenting an aristo in the most perfect disguise. He had a keen sense of humour and it was well worth hanging round that West Barricade in order to see him catch an aristo in the very act of trying to flee from the vengeance of the people.

Sometimes Bibot would let his prey actually out by the gates, allowing him to think for the space of two minutes at least that he had really escaped out of Paris and might even manage to reach the coast of England in safety; but

Bibot would let the unfortunate wretch walk about ten metres towards the open country, then he would send two men after him and bring him back stripped of his disguise.

On this fine afternoon in September, Bibot was sitting on an overturned and empty cask close by the gate of the barricade; a small detachment of citizen soldiers were under his command. The work had been very hot lately. Those cursed aristos were becoming terrified and tried their hardest to slip out of Paris. They were all traitors and right food for the guillotine. Every day Bibot had had the satisfaction of unmasking some fugitive royalists and sending them back to be tried by the Committee of Public Safety presided over by that good patriot Citizen Foucquier Tinville.

The great revolutionary leaders Robespierre and Danton both had commended Bibot for his work and he was proud of the fact that he had sent at least fifty aristos to the guillotine.

But today all the sergeants in command at the various barricades had had special orders. Recently a very great number of aristos had succeeded in escaping out of France and reaching England in safety. There were curious rumours about these escapes; they had become very frequent and very daring; the people's minds were becoming strangely excited about it all. One of the sergeants had been sent to the guillotine for allowing a whole family of aristos to slip out of the North Gate under his very nose.

It was said that these escapes were organized by a band of daring young Englishmen under the leadership of a man who was renowned for his boldness and bravery. No one had seen these mysterious Englishmen but Citizen Foucquier Tinville would sometimes receive a scrap of paper while he was on his way to the sitting of the Committee of Public Safety. Sometimes he would find it in a pocket of his coat or perhaps it would be handed to him while he was passing through a crowd. The paper always contained a brief notice that the band of Englishmen were at work, and it was always

9

signed with a device drawn in red – a little star-shaped flower, which we in England call the Scarlet Pimpernel. Within a few hours of receiving this impudent notice, the citizens of the Committee of Public Safety would hear that a number of royalists and aristocrats had succeeded in reaching the coast, and were on their way to England and safety.

The guards at the gates had been doubled, the sergeants in command had been threatened with death, while rich rewards were offered for the capture of these daring and impudent Englishmen. There was a sum of five thousand francs promised to the man who laid hands on their leader – the mysterious and elusive Scarlet Pimpernel as he became known.

Everyone felt that Bibot would be that man and he thought they were right. Day after day people came to watch him at the West Gate, so as to be present when he laid hands on any fugitive aristo who might be accompanied by the mysterious Englishman.

The sun was sinking low in the west. Bibot prepared himself to close the gates.

"Let the carts come forward," he said.

Some dozen covered carts were drawn up in a row, ready to leave town, in order to fetch the produce from the country close by, for market next morning. They were mostly well known to Bibot, as they went through his gate twice every day on their way to and from the town. He spoke to one or two of their drivers – mostly women – and was at great pains to examine the inside of the carts.

"You never know," he would say, "and I'm not going to be caught like that fool in charge of the North Gate."

The women who drove the carts usually spent their day on the Place de la Grève, beneath the platform of the guillotine, knitting and gossiping, whilst they watched the rows of tumbrils arriving with the victims the Reign of Terror claimed every day. During the day, Bibot had been on duty on the Place. He recognized most of the old hags, knitting-women as they were called, who sat there and knitted while head after head fell beneath the knife, and they themselves got quite bespattered with the blood of those cursed aristos.

"Now then, Mother," said Bibot to one of these horrible hags, "what have you got there?"

He had seen her earlier in the day, with her knitting and the whip of her cart close beside her. Now she had fastened a row of curly locks to the whip handle, all colours, from gold to silver, fair to dark, and she stroked them with her huge, bony fingers as she laughed at Bibot.

"I made friends with Madame Guillotine's lover," she said with a coarse laugh, "he cut these off for me from the heads as they rolled down. He has promised me some more tomorrow, but I don't know if I shall be at my usual place."

"Ah! how is that, Mother?" asked Bibot, who, hardened soldier though he was, could not help shuddering at this loathsome creature, with a ghastly trophy on the handle of her whip.

"My grandson has got the smallpox," she said with a jerk of her thumb towards the inside of her cart; "some say it's the plague. If it is, I shan't be allowed to come into Paris tomorrow."

At the first mention of the word smallpox, Bibot had stepped hastily backwards, and when the old hag spoke of the plague, he retreated from her as fast as he could.

"Curse you!" he muttered, while the whole crowd hastily avoided the cart, leaving it standing all alone in the midst of the place.

"Curse you, citizen, for being a coward," said the old hag. "Bah! what a man to be afraid of sickness."

"Get out with you and with your plague-stricken brood!" shouted Bibot, hoarsely.

And with another rough laugh and coarse jest, the old hag whipped up her lean nag and drove her cart out of the gate.

11

The incident had spoiled the afternoon. The people were terrified of the two illnesses which nothing could cure – smallpox and the plague. They hung about eyeing one another suspiciously as if the plague already lurked in their midst. Presently a captain of the guard appeared suddenly. But he was known to Bibot and there was no fear of his turning out to be a sly Englishman in disguise.

"A cart . . ." he shouted breathlessly, even before he had reached the gates.

"What cart?" asked Bibot, roughly.

"Driven by an old hag . . . A cart . . . A covered cart . . ."

"There were a dozen . . ."

"An old hag who said her grandson had the plague?"

"Yes . . ."

"You have not let them go?"

Bibot's purple cheeks had suddenly become white with fear.

"The cart contained the former Comtesse de Tournay and her two children, all of them traitors and condemned to death."

"And their driver?" muttered Bibot as a shudder ran down his spine.

"Holy Thunder," said the captain, "but it is feared that it was the accursed Englishman himself – the Scarlet Pimpernel."

CHAPTER 2

Dover: The Fisherman's Rest

In the kitchen Sally was extremely busy – saucepans and frying pans were standing in rows on the gigantic hearth, the huge stockpot stood in a corner and the spit turned with slow deliberation, and presented alternately to the glow every side of a noble sirloin of beef. The two little kitchen-maids bustled around, eager to help, hot and panting, with cotton sleeves well tucked up above their dimpled elbows, and giggling over some private jokes of their own whenever Miss Sally's back was turned for a moment. And old Jemima stolid in temper and solid in bulk, kept up a long and subdued grumble, while she stirred the stockpot methodically over the fire.

"What ho, Sally!" called a cheerful but none too musical voice from the coffee room close by. A sound of pewter mugs, tapped with impatient hands on tables could be heard.

"Lud bless my soul!" exclaimed Sally with a good-hum-oured laugh. "What be they all wanting now, I wonder!"

"Beer of course," grumbled Jemima, "you don't expect Jimmy Pitkin to 'ave done with one tankard, do ye?"

"Mr 'Arry, 'e looked uncommon thirsty too," simpered Martha, one of the little kitchenmaids, catching the eye of her companion, and they both giggled.

"I do think Father might get the beer for them," muttered Sally, as Jemima took a couple of foam-crowned jugs from the shelf and began filling up a number of pewter tankards with some of the home-brewed ale for which The Fisherman's Rest had been famous since the days of King Charles. "'E knows how busy we are in 'ere." She went to the small mirror which hung in a corner of the kitchen, hastily smoothed her hair and set her frilled cap at its most becoming angle over her dark curls. Then she took up the tankards by their han-dles, three in each hand, and laughing, grumbling, blushing, carried them through into the coffee room.

The coffee room of The Fisherman's Rest was an old place, even then in 1792. The oak rafters and beams were already black with age – as were the panelled seats with their tall backs, and the long polished tables between, on which innumerable pewter tankards had left fantastic patterns of many-sized rings. In the leaded window, high up, a row of

13

pots of scarlet geraniums and blue larkspur gave the bright note of colour against the dull background of the oak.

Mr Jellyband, landlord of The Fisherman's Rest at Dover was a prosperous man. The pewter on the fine old dressers, the brass above the gigantic hearth, shone like gold and silver – the red-tiled floor was as brilliant as the scarlet geranium on the windowsill – this meant that his servants were good and plentiful, that he had regular customers and kept up the coffee room to a high standard of elegance and order.

As Sally came in, laughing through her frowns, and displaying a row of dazzling white teeth, she was greeted with shouts and chorus of applause.

"Why, here's Sally! What ho, Sally! Hurrah for pretty Sally!"

"I thought you'd grown deaf in that kitchen of yours," muttered Jimmy Pitkin, as he passed the back of his hand across his very dry lips. But, as she put down the newly filled tankards, Sally had eyes only for a young man with fair curly hair and seemed in no hurry to get back to her pots and pans.

Pacing the hearth, his legs wide apart, a long clay pipe in his mouth, stood mine host himself, worthy Mr Jellyband, landlord of The Fisherman's Rest, as his father had been before him, and his grandfather and great-grandfather too. Portly in build, jovial in countenance and somewhat bald, Mr Jellyband was a typical rural John Bull, proud to be an Englishman and thinking nothing of foreigners.

Mr Jellyband wore the typical scarlet waistcoat, with shiny brass buttons, the corduroy breeches, the grey worsted stockings, and smart buckled shoes that were customary for every self-respecting innkeeper in Great Britain in these days – and while pretty, motherless Sally needed four pairs of hands to do all the work that fell on her shoulders, worthy Mr Jellyband discussed the affairs of nations with his most privileged guests.

The coffee room, indeed, lighted by two well-polished

lamps, which hung from the raftered ceiling, looked cheerful and cosy. Through the dense clouds of tobacco that hung about in every corner the faces of Mr Jellyband's customers appeared red and pleasant to look at and on good terms with themselves, their host and all the world. There was plenty of laughing and cheerful conversation, not of a very learned sort. Sally's giggles showed that Mr Harry Waite was making good use of the short time she could spare him.

They were mostly fisherfolk who patronized Mr Jellyband's coffee room, but fishermen are known to be very thirsty people; the salt which they breath in, when they are on the sea, accounts for their parched throats when on shore. But The Fisherman's Rest was something more than a meeting-place for those humble folk. The London and Dover coach started from the hostel daily, and passengers who crossed the Channel in either direction all became acquainted with Mr Jellyband, his French wines and his home-brewed ales.

It was towards the close of September 1792, and the weather, which had been brilliant and hot throughout the month, had suddenly broken up; for two days torrents of rain had deluged the south of England, doing its level best to ruin what chances the apples and pears and late plums had of becoming really fine fruit. Even now it was beating against the leaded windows, and tumbling down the chimney, making the cheerful wood fire sizzle in the hearth.

"Lud! Did you ever see such a wet September, Mr Jellyband?" asked Mr Hempseed. He sat in one of the seats inside the hearth, did Mr Hempseed, for he was an important personage, of some seventy-five years and much favoured by Mr Jellyband for political discussions. With one hand buried in the capacious pockets of his corduroys underneath his elaborately worked well-worn smock, the other holding his long clay pipe, Mr Hempseed sat there looking dejectedly across the room at the rivulets of moisture which trickled down the windowpanes.

15

"No," replied Mr Jellyband solemnly. "I dunno, Mr 'Empseed, as ever I did." A giggle came from across the room where Sally was still dallying with Mr Harry.

"Now Sally," said her father frowning, "go and get on with my Lord Tony's supper, for, if it ain't the best we can do, and 'e's not satisfied, see what you'll get, that's all."

Reluctantly Sally obeyed.

"Is you expecting special guests then tonight, Mr Jellyband?" asked Jimmy Pitkin.

"Aye, that I be," replied Jellyband, "friends of my Lord Tony himself. Dukes and duchesses from over the water yonder, whom the young lord and his friend Sir Andrew Ffoulkes, and other noblemen have helped out of the clutches of them murderin' French devils."

Two quiet strangers were sitting in the corner and one of them rose and came up to Mr Jellyband.

"Well, my honest friend," he said cheerfully, "I can see that you would be a match for any twenty Frenchmen, and here's to your very good health, my worthy host, if you'll do me the honour to finish this bottle of wine with me."

"I am sure you're very polite, sir," said Mr Jellyband, "and I don't mind if I do."

The stranger poured out a couple of tankards full of wine, and having offered one to mine host, he took the other himself.

"Loyal Englishmen as we all are," he said, while a humorous smile played round the corners of his thin lips – "loyal as we are, we must admit that this at least is one good thing that comes to us from France."

"Aye, we'll none of us deny that, sir," said his host.

"And here's to the best landlord in England, our worthy host, Mr Jellyband," said the stranger in a loud tone of voice. Clapping and cheering greeted this toast and the quiet gentleman went back to his friend.

CHAPTER 3

The Refugees

Feelings in every part of England certainly ran very high at this time against the French and their doings. Smugglers and lawful traders between the French and English coasts brought snatches of news from over the water, which made every honest Englishman's blood boil, and made him long to have "a good go" at those murderers, who had imprisoned their king and all his family, treated the queen and the royal children shamefully, and were even now loudly demanding the blood of the whole Bourbon family and of every one of its supporters.

The execution of the Princesse de Lamballe, Marie Antoinette's young and charming friend, had filled everyone in England with unspeakable horror, the daily execution of scores of royalists of good family, whose only sin was their aristocratic name, seemed to cry for vengeance to the whole of civilized Europe. Yet, with all that, no one dared to interfere and the British Government did not feel that the country was fit to embark on a hard and costly war.

But now Sally came running back, very excited and very eager. The joyous company in the coffee room had heard nothing of the noise outside, but she had spied a dripping horse and rider who had stopped at the door of The Fisherman's Rest, and while the stable boy ran forward to take charge of the horse, pretty Sally went to the front door to greet the welcome visitor.

"I think I saw my Lord Anthony's horse out in the yard, Father," she said, as she ran across the coffee room.

17

But already the door had been thrown open from outside, and the next moment an arm, dripping with the heavy rain, was round pretty Sally's waist, while a hearty voice echoed along the polished rafters of the coffee room.

"Bless your brown eyes for being so sharp, my pretty Sally," said the man who had just entered, while worthy Mr Jellyband came bustling forward, eager, alert and fussy to greet one of his most favoured guests.

"Lud, I protest, Sally," added Lord Anthony as he planted a kiss on Miss Sally's blooming cheeks, "but you are growing prettier and prettier every time I see you – and my honest friend, Jellyband here, must have hard work to keep the fellows off that slim waist of yours. What say you, Mr Waite?"

Mr Waite did not like that particular type of joke, but he respected Lord Anthony and only replied with a doubtful grunt.

Lord Anthony Dewhurst, one of the sons of the Duke of Exeter, was a fine type of young English gentleman – tall, well set-up, broad of shoulders and merry of face, his laughter rang loudly wherever he went. A good sportsman, a lively companion, a courteous well-bred man of the world, with not too much brains to spoil his temper, he was a favourite in London drawing rooms or in the coffee rooms of village inns. At The Fisherman's Rest everyone knew him – for he was fond of a trip across to France, and always spent a night under Mr Jellyband's roof on his way there or back.

He nodded to Waite, Pitkin and the others as he at last released Sally's waist, and crossed over to the hearth to warm and dry himself: as he did so, he cast a quick, somewhat suspicious glance at the two strangers, who had quietly resumed their game of dominoes, and for a moment a look of anxiety clouded his cheerful young face.

But only for a moment: the next he had turned to Mr Hempseed, who was respectfully touching his forelock.

"Well, Mr Hempseed, and how is the fruit?"

"Badly, my lord, badly," replied Mr Hempseed dolefully,

"but what can you expect when this 'ere government does nothing about them rascals in France who are murdering the nobility and anyone who doesn't agree with them and their ideas?"

"Those they can get hold of, they do, but we have got some friends coming here tonight, who have escaped their clutches," replied Lord Anthony.

"Thanks to you, my lord, and to your friends, so I've heard it said," said Mr Jellyband.

Lord Anthony's hand fell warningly on his arm as he looked quickly towards the strangers.

"They are all right, my lord," said Mr Jellyband. "I wouldn't have said what I did if I didn't think we were among friends."

"That's all right then, if we are among friends," said Lord Anthony. "But tell me, you have no one else staying here, have you?"

"No my lord, Sir Percy Blakeney and his lady will be here presently, but they're not going to stay."

"Lady Blakeney?" queried Lord Anthony, in some astonishment.

"Aye, my lord. Sir Percy's skipper was here just now. He says that my lady's brother is crossing over to France today in the *Day Dream*, which is Sir Percy's yacht, and Sir Percy and my lady will come with him as far as here to see the last of him. It don't put you out, do it, my lord?"

"No, it doesn't put me out, friend; nothing will put me out, unless that supper is not the very best which Miss Sally can cook, and which has ever been served in The Fisherman's Rest."

"You need have no fear of that, my lord," said Sally, who all this while had been busy setting the table for supper. And very inviting it looked, with a large bunch of brilliantly coloured dahlias in the centre, and the bright pewter goblets and blue china about.

"How many shall I lay for, my lord?"

"Five places, pretty Sally, but let the supper be enough for ten at least – our friends will be tired, and, I hope, hungry. As for me, I vow I could demolish a baron of beef tonight."

"Here they are, I do believe," said Sally excitedly, as a distant clatter of horses and wheels could now be distinctly heard, drawing rapidly nearer.

There was general commotion in the coffee room. Everyone was curious to see my Lord Anthony's swell friends from over the water. Only the two strangers in the corner did not share in the general excitement. They were calmly finishing their game of dominoes, and did not even look once towards the door.

"Straight ahead, Comtesse, the door on your right," said a pleasant voice outside.

The door was thrown wide open and Mr Jellyband, bowing profusely, ushered two ladies and two gentlemen into the coffee room.

"Welcome! Welcome to old England!" said Lord Anthony, as he came eagerly forward with both hands outstretched towards the newcomers.

"Ah, you are Lord Anthony Dewhurst, I think," said one of the ladies, speaking with a strong foreign accent.

"At your service, Madame," he replied, as he ceremoniously kissed the hands of both the ladies, then turned to the men and shook them warmly by the hand.

Sally was already helping the ladies to take off their travelling cloaks, and both turned, with a shiver, towards the brightly blazing hearth.

"Ah, Messieurs! What can I say?" said the elder of the two ladies, as she stretched a pair of fine, aristocratic hands to the warmth of the blaze, and looked gratefully first at Lord Anthony, then at one of the young men who had accompanied her party, and who was busy taking off his heavy, caped coat.

"Only that you are glad to be in England, Comtesse," replied Lord Anthony, "and that you have not suffered too much from your trying voyage."

20

"Indeed, indeed, we are glad to be in England," she said, while her eyes filled with tears, "and we have forgotten already all that we have suffered."

Her voice was musical and low, and her handsome face was marked by suffering. Her snow-white hair was dressed high above the forehead, after the fashion of the times.

"I hope my friend, Sir Andrew Ffoulkes, proved an entertaining travelling companion, Madame."

"Sir Andrew was kindness itself. How could my children and I ever show enough gratitude to you all, Messieurs?"

Her daughter, a dainty, girlish figure with a sweet face, looked pathetically tired and sorrowful. She had said nothing as yet, but her eyes, large, brown and full of tears looked up from the fire and saw Sir Andrew Ffoulkes looking down at her with unconcealed admiration.

A little colour rushed up to her pale cheeks.

"So this is England," she said, as she looked round with childlike curiosity at the open hearth, the oak rafters, and the country folk with their elaborate smocks and jolly, ruddy faces.

"A bit of it, Mademoiselle," replied Sir Andrew, smiling, "but all of it at your service."

The young girl blushed again, but this time a bright smile was on her face. She said nothing, and Sir Andrew, too was silent, but they understood each other.

At that moment, Sally appeared in the doorway carrying a gigantic tureen from which rose a cloud of steam and an abundance of savoury odour.

Lord Anthony offered his arm to the Comtesse and led her to the supper table. There was general bustle in the coffee-room. Most of the country and fisherfolk had gone to make way for the newcomers and were smoking their pipes elsewhere. Only the two strangers stayed on, quietly playing their game of dominoes and sipping their wine, while at another table Harry Waite was fast losing his temper, for he did not like the way the Comtesse's young son, the Vicomte de Tournay, was staring at Sally.

He was scarce nineteen, a beardless boy, elegantly dressed and seemingly untouched by the terrible events in his own country. If all the girls in England were like Miss Sally, he would be well satisfied.

Lord Anthony had already sat down at the head of the table, with the Comtesse on his right. Jellyband was bustling round filling glasses and putting chairs straight. Sally waited, ready to serve the soup. Mr Harry Waite's friends had at last succeeded in taking him out of the room, for his temper was growing more and more violent under the Vicomte's obvious admiration for Sally.

"Suzanne," came in stern, commanding accents from the Comtesse.

Her daughter blushed again; she had lost count of time and of place, while she stood before the fire, allowing the handsome young Englishman's eyes to dwell upon her sweet face and his hand to rest upon hers. Her mother's voice brought her back to reality once more and with a quick "Yes, Mama," she took her place at the supper table.

CHAPTER 4

The League of the Scarlet Pimpernel

They all looked a happy party as they sat round the table; Sir Andrew Ffoulkes and Lord Anthony Dewhurst, two good-looking well-bred Englishmen and the aristocratic Comtesse with her two children, just escaped from fearful danger and safe at last on the shores of protecting England.

In the corner the two strangers had apparently finished their game. One of them stood up, and standing with his back to the merry company at the table, he slowly pulled on his top coat with its three capes. As he did so, he gave one quick glance all round him. Everyone was busy laughing and chatting, and he murmured the words "All Safe!" At this, his companion slipped to his knees and, without a sound, crept under the oak bench. The stranger then with a loud "Goodnight" quietly walked out of the coffee room.

Not one of those at the supper table had noticed but when the stranger closed the door behind him, they all sighed with relief.

"Alone, at last!" said Lord Anthony.

Then the young Vicomte de Tournay rose, glass in hand. He raised it aloft, and said in broken English –

"To His Majesty George III of England. God bless him for his hospitality to us all, poor exiles from France."

"His Majesty the King!" echoed Lord Anthony and Sir Andrew, as they drank loyally to the toast.

"To His Majesty King Louis of France," added Sir Andrew solemnly, "may God protect him, and give him victory over his enemies."

Everyone rose and drank this toast in silence. The King of France was a prisoner of his own people and they feared what his fate might be.

"And to Monsieur le Comte de Tournay de Basserive," said Lord Anthony, merrily. "May we welcome him in England before many days are over."

"Oh, Monsieur," said the Comtesse, as with a slightly trembling hand she put her glass to her lips. "I scarcely dare to hope. I should not have left him but my children refused to go without me."

Lord Anthony had now served out the soup, and for the next few minutes all conversation ceased, while Jellyband and Sally handed round the plates, and everyone began to eat.

But the poor Comtesse took little and presently started crying gently to herself. Suzanne went over to her and tried to kiss away her tears. Then, looking through a wealth of brown curls across at Sir Andrew, she said, "As for me, Monsieur, I trust you absolutely, and I know that you will bring my dear father safely to England, just as you brought us today."

"Mademoiselle," replied Sir Andrew, "my life is at your service, but I am only a humble tool in the hands of our great leader, who organized your escape."

"Your leader?" said the Comtesse eagerly. "Of course, you must have a leader. Where is he? I must go to him and thank him for all that he has done for us."

"Alas, Madame," said Lord Anthony, "that is impossible."

"Impossible? – Why?"

"Because the Scarlet Pimpernel works in secret and his identity is only known to his closest followers."

"The Scarlet Pimpernel?" said Suzanne. "What a funny name! What is the Scarlet Pimpernel, Monsieur?"

"The Scarlet Pimpernel," said Sir Andrew, his eyes shining, "is the name of a humble English wayside flower, but it is also the name chosen to hide the identity of the best and bravest man in all the world, so that he may carry out the noble task which he has set himself to do."

"Ah yes," said the young Vicomte. "I have heard of this Scarlet Pimpernel. It is a little red flower – yes? They say in Paris that every time a royalist escapes to England that devil, Foucquier Tinville, the Public Prosecutor, receives a paper with that little flower traced in red upon it. Is that so?"

"That is so," agreed Lord Anthony.

"Then he will have received one such paper today."

"Undoubtedly. It is excellent sport as you can imagine!"

The Comtesse shook her head. She could not understand why these young men and their great leader should run such terrible risks. Anyone caught sheltering or assisting suspected royalists would be condemned and executed themselves. The fact that they were English would not save them once they were in France.

With a shudder, she recalled the events of the last few days, her escape from Paris with her two children, all three of them hidden beneath the hood of a rickety cart, and lying among a heap of turnips and cabbages, not daring to breath, while the mob howled, "Kill the aristos" at that awful West Barricade.

It had all occurred in such a miraculous way: she and her husband knew that they had been placed on the list of "suspected persons", which meant that their trial and death was but a matter of days – of hours perhaps. Then came hope; they received a note signed with the emblem of the

Scarlet Pimpernel which gave them clear instructions. The Comtesse had to take the children and leave her husband. There was a hope of reunion – but the poor wife's heart was torn in two. They escaped in a covered cart driven by a ghastly old woman with a victim's curls on her whip handle.

Then they were rescued by these brave young Englishmen who had risked their lives to save them, as they had already saved scores of innocent people. And all for sport? She did not believe it and neither did Suzanne as her eyes met those of brave Sir Andrew.

"How many are there in your league, Monsieur?" she asked shyly.

"Twenty all told, Mademoiselle," he replied, "one to command and nineteen to obey. All of us Englishmen, and all under promise to obey our leader and to rescue the innocent."

"May God protect you all," said the Comtesse, fervently.

"He has done that so far, Madame."

"You are so brave, so devoted to your fellow men, but in France it is all treachery and all in the name of liberty and fraternity."

"And the women are worse than the men, more bitter against us aristocrats," said the Vicomte with a sigh.

"Ah yes," added the Comtesse, bitterly, "there was that woman, Marguerite St Just, for instance. She denounced the Marquis de St Cyr and all his family to the awful tribunal of the Terror."

"Marguerite St Just?" said Lord Anthony, looking quickly across at Andrew, "surely not!"

"Yes," replied the Comtesse, "you must know her. She was a leading actress of the Comédie Française, and she married an Englishman lately."

"Know her?" said Lord Anthony. "Know Lady Blakeney – the most fashionable woman in London – the wife of the richest man in England? Of course we all know Lady Blakeney."

"She was a schoolfellow of mine at the convent in Paris," said Suzanne, "and we came over to England together to learn your language. I was very fond of Marguerite, and I cannot believe that she ever did anything so wicked."

"It certainly seems incredible," said Sir Andrew. "You say that she actually denounced the Marquis de St Cyr? Why should she have done such a thing? Surely there must be some mistake —"

"No mistake is possible, Monsieur," rejoined the Comtesse, coldly. "Marguerite St Just's brother is a well-known Republican. There was some talk of a family feud between him and the Marquis de St Cyr. The Marquis was my cousin; the St Justs are not of good family and the Republican Government employs many spies. I assure you there is no mistake. You have not heard this story?"

"Faith, Madame, I did hear some vague rumours of it, but in England no one would believe it. Sir Percy Blakeney, her husband, is a very wealthy man of high social position, the close friend of the Prince of Wales and Lady Blakeney leads both fashion and society in London."

"That may be, Monsieur, and we shall, of course, lead a very quiet life in England, but I pray God that while I remain in this beautiful country I may never meet Marguerite St Just."

A hush fell over the table. Suzanne looked sad and silent. Sir Andrew fidgeted uneasily with his fork, while the Comtesse sat, rigid and unbending, in her straight-backed chair. As for Sir Anthony, he looked extremely uncomfortable, and glanced once or twice towards Jellyband who looked just as uncomfortable as he did.

"At what time do you expect Sir Percy and Lady Blakeney?" he managed to whisper to mine host.

"Any moment, my lord," whispered Jellyband in reply.

Even as he spoke, a distant clatter was heard of an

approaching coach: louder and louder it grew, one or two shouts were heard, then came the rattle of horses' hoofs on the uneven cobblestones, and the next moment a stable boy had thrown open the coffee room door and rushed in excitedly.

"Sir Percy Blakeney and my lady," he shouted at the top of his voice, "they're just arriving."

And with more shouting, jingling of harness, and iron hoofs upon the stones, a magnificent coach, drawn by four superb bays, had halted outside the porch of The Fisherman's Rest.

CHAPTER 5

Marguerite

In a moment the coffee room became the scene of hopeless confusion and disorder. Lord Anthony had jumped up from his seat and was giving instructions to poor Mr Jellyband who seemed at his wits' end what to do.

"For goodness' sake, man," said his lordship, "try to keep Lady Blakeney talking outside for a moment while the ladies leave the room."

"Quick, Sally! The candles!" shouted Jellyband, running around and adding to the general muddle.

The Comtesse had risen to her feet and, standing rigid and erect, she repeated mechanically –

"I will not see her! I will not see her!"

Voices were heard outside, including one low, sweet one with a slight foreign accent. Everyone in the coffee room heard it. Sally was holding the candles by the opposite door which led to the bedrooms upstairs, and the Comtesse was about to make a hasty retreat before the enemy who

28

owned such a sweet, musical voice. Suzanne was reluctantly preparing to follow her mother, but at the same time she was casting regretful glances towards the door, where she hoped still to see her dearly loved former schoolfellow.

Jellyband threw open the door.

"Suzanne, come with me at once," said the Comtesse.

"Oh Mama!" pleaded Suzanne.

"Welcome my lady," said Mr Jellyband in feeble tones, as he stood clumsily trying to bar the way.

"Heavens, my good man," said Lady Blakeney, with some impatience, "why are you standing in my way, dancing about like a turkey with a sore foot? Let me get to the fire; I am wet and perished with the cold."

And the next moment Lady Blakeney gently pushing mine host on one side, had swept into the coffee room.

There are many portraits and miniatures of Marguerite St Just, now Lady Blakeney, but it is doubtful if any of these do her justice. She was tall over the average and bore herself like royalty. She was barely five-and-twenty and her beauty was at its most dazzling stage. Her auburn hair was free of powder and her large hat with its waving plumes threw a soft shadow across her handsome face.

Marguerite Blakeney wore a rich blue velvet robe which showed off her graceful figure and in her tiny hand she held the tall stick adorned with a large bunch of ribbons which fashionable ladies of that period had taken to wearing recently.

She gave a quick glance round the room, nodded pleasantly to Sir Andrew Ffoulkes and held out her hand to Lord Tony.

"Hello, my Lord Tony, what are *you* doing here in Dover?" she said merrily.

Then, without waiting for a reply, she turned and faced the Comtesse and Suzanne. Her whole face lighted up as she stretched out both arms towards the young girl.

"Why if that isn't my little Suzanne over there! How came you to be in England? And Madame too!"

She went over with arms outstretched, seeming not to realize that as the sister of Armand St Just, an ardent Republican who had brought about the downfall of the St Cyr family she would not be welcome. Her brother was a moderate man but had a feud with the ancient family and no outsiders knew the reason.

"Suzanne, I forbid you to speak to that woman," said the Comtesse sternly, placing her hand upon her daughter's arm.

She had spoken in English, so that all might hear and understand – the two young Englishmen as well as the innkeeper and his daughter. Mr Jellyband and Sally were horrified that a foreigner should insult her ladyship, who was English, now that she was Sir Percy's wife and a friend of the Princess of Wales as well.

As for Lord Anthony and Sir Andrew Ffoulkes, their very hearts seemed to stand still and both glanced hurriedly towards the door, from where a slow, drawly, not unpleasant voice had already been heard.

Marguerite's face had become as white as the soft lace which swathed her throat, and the hand which held the tall, beribboned stick was clenched and trembled somewhat. Then, with her clear blue eyes, she looked straight at the rigid Comtesse, shrugged her shoulders and said gaily, "Hoity-toity, citizeness, what fly stings you pray?"

"We are in England now, Madame," replied the Comtesse, coldly, "and I am at liberty to forbid my daughter to touch your hand in friendship. Come, Suzanne."

She beckoned to her daughter, and without another look at Marguerite Blakeney, but with a deep, old-fashioned curtsey to the two young men, she sailed majestically out of the room.

There was silence in the old inn parlour for a moment, as the rustle of the Comtesse's skirts died away down the passage. Marguerite, rigid as a statue, looked stony-faced at the upright figure as it disappeared through the doorway – but as little Suzanne, humble and obedient, was about to follow her mother, the hard, set expression suddenly vanished, and a wistful, almost pathetic look stole into Marguerite's eyes . . .

Suzanne saw the look; she turned at the door, ran back and, putting her arms round Marguerite, kissed her warmly. Then she followed her mother. Sally went behind them with a final curtsey to my lady.

"La," said Lady Blakeney, apparently forgetting that the son was still in the room, "did you ever see such an unpleasant person? I hope when I grow old I shan't look like that."

The young Vicomte took a step forward as if to defend his mother but before he could say a word, a pleasant, though rather silly laugh was heard from outside, and the next moment an unusually tall and very richly dressed figure appeared in the doorway.

CHAPTER 6

Sir Percy

Sir Percy Blakeney was, in this year of grace, still a year or two on the right side of thirty. Tall, above the average, broad-shouldered and massively built, he would have been called unusually good-looking, but for a certain lazy expression in his deep-set blue eyes, and that perpetual silly laugh which came surprisingly from a strong, clearly cut mouth.

It was nearly a year ago now that Sir Percy Blakeney, Baronet, one of the richest men in England and close friend of the Prince of Wales, had astonished fashionable society in

London and Bath by bringing home from one of his journeys abroad a beautiful, fascinating, clever, French wife. He, a sleepy, dull most British of Britishers, had won her hand in the face of countless competitors.

Marguerite St Just was just eighteen when she made her début in artistic Parisian circles at the very moment when the beginnings of the greatest social upheaval the world at that time had ever known – the Revolution was taking place.

Under the protection of a young and devoted brother, she had soon gathered round her in her charming apartment in the Rue Richelieu a group of brilliant friends. Marguerite St Just was a Republican, but she was not interested in the differences between rich and poor. She judged people only by their brains. Clever men, distinguished men, and even men of high position gathered round the fascinating young actress of the Comédie Française, and she glided through republican, revolutionary, bloodthirsty Paris like a shining comet, with a trail behind her of the most distinguished, most interesting men in Europe.

Then one fine day she married Sir Percy Blakeney. Some said she did it for his money, but those who knew her laughed to scorn the idea that she had married a fool for the sake of his worldly goods. They knew, as a matter of fact, that Marguerite St Just cared nothing about money and still less about a title, yet she chose Sir Percy. London Society thought that, in spite of his wealth and friendship with the Prince of Wales, he was totally unsuited to wed such a brilliant and witty wife.

Sir Percy had spent most of his early life abroad. His father, Sir Algernon Blakeney, idolized his young wife, but had the terrible misfortune of seeing her become hopelessly insane after two years of happy married life following the birth of her son. He took his family out of the country and Percy grew up between a sick mother and a distracted father until he came of age. The death of his parents came soon afterwards, close upon one another, and he was left a free man. The family had led a simple and retired life and so the large Blakeney fortune had increased tenfold.

Sir Percy Blakeney had travelled a great deal abroad, before he brought home his beautiful young French wife. Society was ready to receive them with open arms. Sir Percy was rich, his wife was intelligent and accomplished, the Prince of Wales took a very great liking to them both.

In his beautiful house at Richmond, Sir Percy cheerfully played second fiddle to his attractive wife, lavishing jewels and luxuries upon her while she dispensed the hospitality of his superb mansion with the same graciousness with which she had welcomed her clever friends in Paris.

Sir Percy, handsome as ever and perfectly dressed in spite of the rain and mud, had strolled into the old inn parlour, shaking the wet off his fine overcoat; then putting up a gold-rimmed eyeglass to his lazy blue eye, he surveyed the company, upon whom an embarrassed silence had suddenly fallen.

"How do, Tony! How do, Ffoulkes?" he said, shaking the two young men by the hand. "Did you ever see such a beastly day? Demmed climate this."

With a quaint little laugh, Marguerite had turned towards her husband, and was surveying him from head to foot, with an amused little twinkle in her merry blue eyes.

"La!" said Sir Percy, after a moment or two's silence, as no one spoke, "How uncomfortable you all look ... What's up?"

"Nothing Sir Percy," said Marguerite, forcing a smile "– only an insult to your wife." She laughed as she said this and he was apparently reassured. "La, m'dear," he answered placidly, "and who was the bold man who dared to tackle *you*, eh?"

Lord Tony tried to say something, but had no time to do so, for the young Vicomte had already quickly stepped forward and made an elaborate bow. "Monsieur," he said speaking in broken English, "my mother, the Comtesse de

33

Tournay de Basserive, has offended Madame, who, I see, is your wife. I cannot ask your pardon for my mother; what she does is right in my eyes. But I am able to offer you the usual satisfaction between men of honour."

The slim young man drew himself up to his full height and looked very enthusiastic, very proud, and very hot as he gazed at the six foot of Sir Percy Blakeney in all his gorgeousness.

"Lud, Sir Andrew," said Marguerite, with one of her merry infectious laughs, "look at that pretty picture – the English turkey and the French bantam." The comparison was quite perfect, and the English turkey looked down with complete bewilderment upon the dainty little French bantam, which hovered quite threateningly around him.

"Monsieur," said the young man, "I fear you have not understood. I offer you the only possible satisfaction among gentlemen."

"What the devil is that?" asked Sir Percy calmly.

"My sword, Monsieur," replied the Vicomte who was beginning to lose his temper.

"Lud love you, sir," muttered Sir Percy, turning away, "what's the good of your sword to me?"

"A duel, Monsieur," stammered the Vicomte, his voice choking with anger.

"A duel, sir? Is that what you mean? Odd's fish, you are a bloodthirsty young ruffian. Do you want to make a hole in a law-abiding man? I never fight duels, sir. Uncomfortable things, duels, aren't they Tony?"

"Sir Percy is in the right, Vicomte," said Lord Anthony, laying a friendly hand on the young Frenchman's shoulder. "And it would hardly be right that you should commence your career in England by provoking him to a duel."

For a moment longer the Vicomte hesitated, then with a slight shrug of the shoulders, he said with becoming dignity – "Ah, well! If Monsieur is satisfied, I have no griefs. You are our protector. If I have done wrong, I withdraw myself."

34

"Aye, do!" replied Blakeney, with a long sigh of satisfaction, "withdraw yourself over there. Demmed excitable little puppy," he added under his breath. Then he stood up and said cheerfully, "We must have a bowl to celebrate peace. Hey Jelly!" and he tapped vigorously on the table near him. Mr Jellyband came running.

"A bowl of punch, Jelly, hot and strong, eh?" said Sir Percy.

"Nay, there is no time, Sir Percy," said Marguerite. "The skipper will be here directly and my brother must get on board, or the *Day Dream* will miss the tide."

"I think, your ladyship," said Jellyband respectfully, "that the young gentleman is coming along now with Sir Percy's skipper."

"That's right," said Blakeney, "then Armand can join us in the merry bowl. Perhaps the Vicomte, too, will join us in a glass as a token of reconciliation."

"In fact you are all such merry company," said Marguerite, "that I trust you will forgive me if I bid my brother goodbye in another room."

It would have been bad form to protest. Both Lord Anthony and Sir Andrew felt that Lady Blakeney could not altogether feel in tune with them at that moment. Her love for her brother, Armand St Just, was deep and touching. He had spent a few weeks with her in her English home, and was going back to serve his country, at a time when death was the usual reward for the most enduring loyalty.

Sir Percy made no attempt to detain his wife. He opened the coffee room door for her and made her an elaborate bow, as she sailed out of the room without bestowing on him more than a passing, slightly contemptuous glance. Only Sir Andrew Ffoulkes, whose every thought since he had met Suzanne de Tournay seemed keener, more gentle, more sympathetic, noted the curious look of intense longing, of deep and hopeless passion, with which Sir Percy followed the retreating figure of his wife.

CHAPTER 7

The Secret Orchard

Once outside the noisy coffee room, alone in the dimly lighted passage, Marguerite Blakeney seemed to breathe more freely. She heaved a deep sigh and a few tears fell unheeded down her cheeks.

Outside the rain had ceased, and through the swiftly passing clouds the pale rays of an after-storm sun shone upon the wonderful white coast of Kent and the quaint, irregular houses that clustered round the Admiralty Pier. Marguerite stepped on to the porch and looked out to sea where a graceful schooner, the *Day Dream*, was gently dancing in the breeze. She was waiting to take Armand St Just back to France into the very midst of a seething, bloody revolution.

In the distance two figures were approaching The Fisherman's Rest: one, an oldish man, with a curious fringe of grey hair round a plump and massive chin, and who walked in a peculiar rolling fashion which marked him out as a sailor, the other, a young, slight figure, neatly dressed in a dark, many-caped overcoat; he was clean shaven, and his dark hair was taken well back over a clear and noble forehead.

"Armand!" said Marguerite, as soon as she saw him approaching from the distance, and a happy smile shone on her sweet face, even through the tears.

A minute or two later brother and sister were locked in each other's arms, while the old skipper stood respectfully on one side.

"How much time have we got, Briggs," asked Lady Blakeney, "before Monsieur St Just needs to go on board?"

"We ought to weigh anchor before half an hour, your ladyship," replied the old man, pulling at his grey forelock.

Linking her arm in his, Marguerite led her brother towards the cliffs.

"Half an hour," she said, looking wistfully out to sea, "half an hour more and you'll be far from me, Armand. I can't believe you are going. These last few days – while Percy has been away, and I've had you all to myself have slipped by like a dream."

"I am not going far," said the young man, "a narrow channel to cross – a few miles of road – I can soon come back."

"It is not the distance, Armand, but that awful Paris; it is worse day by day."

"Our own beautiful country, dear," said Armand.

"They are going too far. You are a Republican, so am I. We both believe in liberty and equality, but even you must think that they are going too far."

"Hush!" said Armand, glancing fearfully round him.

"Ah! you see; you don't think it is safe to speak of these things even here, in England." She clung to him suddenly. "Don't go, Armand! Don't go back." Her voice was choked with sobs, her eyes, tender, blue and loving, gazed appealingly at the young man who was looking steadfastly at her.

"You would in any case be my own brave sister," he said gently "who would remember that, when France is in peril, it is not for her sons to turn their backs on her."

"But I have only you to care for me."

"You have Percy. He cares for you."

A look of strange wistfulness crept into her eyes as she murmured, "He did . . . once."

"Listen, Marguerite, there is something I must ask you. I have been wanting to ask you for some time. Does Sir Percy know the part you played in the arrest of the Marquis de St Cyr?"

Marguerite laughed bitterly. "Yes, he does know. I told him after I married him."

"And did he know the full story – that you were not to blame?"

"He heard about it from someone else. It was too late to explain and now I have the satisfaction, Armand, of knowing that the biggest fool in England has the most complete contempt for his wife."

Armand, who loved his sister so dearly, felt that he had placed a somewhat clumsy finger upon an aching wound.

"But Sir Percy loved you," he repeated gently.

"Loved me? – Well, Armand, I thought at one time that he did or I would not have married him. I dare say that even you thought – as everybody else did – that I married him for his wealth – but I assure you, dear, that it was not so. He seemed to worship me and it went straight to my heart. I would have allowed myself to be worshipped and given infinite tenderness in return."

Armand thought he understood. Sir Percy could not understand how someone could denounce a fellow man to a tribunal that knew no pardon and, as his love waned, Marguerite's heart had awakened with love for him.

This was his first visit to England since her marriage, and the few months of separation seemed to have put a thin wall between them; the same love was there on both sides, but each now seemed to have a secret orchard, into which the other dared not penetrate.

There was much Armand St Just could not tell his sister. Things were changing every day in France; she might not understand how his own views might be changing as the deeds of those who had been his friends grew in horror and outrage. And Marguerite could not speak to her brother about the secrets of her heart. She hardly understood them herself and only knew that, in the midst of luxury, she felt lonely and unhappy.

And now Armand was going away; she feared for his

safety, she longed for his presence. She would not spoil these last sad moments together by speaking about herself. She led him gently along the cliffs, then down to the beach; their arms linked. They still had so much to say, that lay just outside that secret orchard of theirs.

CHAPTER 8

The Agent of the Republic

The afternoon was rapidly drawing to a close, and a long, chilly English summer's evening was throwing a misty pall over the green Kentish landscape.

The *Day Dream* had set sail, and Marguerite Blakeney stood alone on the edge of the cliff for over an hour, watching those white sails which bore her beloved brother so swiftly away from her. Sir Percy had thoughtfully left her alone. He was always thoughtful, and generous as well, but his love and devotion seemed to vanish completely when, twenty-four hours after their marriage, she told him of her part in the arrest of the Marquis de St Cyr. Without meaning any harm, she had spoken of certain matters connected with the Marquis in front of some men – her friends – who had used this information against the unfortunate Marquis, and sent him and his family to the guillotine.

Armand himself had nothing to do with the arrests, but it was on his account that Marguerite hated the Marquis. Years ago, Armand had loved his daughter Angèle, but she was the daughter of an aristocrat while he was just one of the people. One day Armand ventured to send a small love poem to the idol of his dreams. The next night he was waylaid just outside Paris by the servants of the Marquis de St Cyr and thrashed within an inch of his life, because he had dared to raise his eyes to the daughter of an aristocrat. This kind of thing was common during the years before the Revolution and led to bloody reprisals later, sending many a proud and haughty nobleman to the guillotine.

Marguerite never forgot what had been done to her brother and when she heard among her friends that the St Cyrs were plotting to obtain the support of the Emperor of Austria in putting down the growing revolution in France, she reported them as traitors without thinking what the consequences would be. Within twenty-four hours, the Marquis was arrested. His papers were searched: letters from the Austrian Emperor, promising to send troops against the people of Paris, were found in his desk. He was charged with treason against the nation, and sent to the guillotine, while his family, his wife and his sons, shared this awful fate.

Marguerite, horrified at the consequences of her own thoughtlessness, was powerless to save them. Her friends, who were the leaders of the revolutionary movement, said she was a heroine and when she married Sir Percy Blakeney, she did not realize what he would think, although she was filled with sorrow for what had happened. She made a full confession to her husband, trusting to his blind love and devotion to her to excuse her in his eyes.

Sir Percy took her admission very quietly, almost as if he had not understood, but, from that time he seemed to have laid aside his love for her. He remained the same, always considerate, always a gentleman. She had all that a wealthy husband can give to a pretty wife, yet on this beautiful summer's evening, with the white sails of the *Day*

41

Dream finally hidden by the evening shadows, she felt more lonely than a poor tramp she saw plodding his way wearily along the rugged cliffs.

With a heavy sigh, she turned her back upon the sea and cliffs, and walked slowly back towards The Fisherman's Rest. As she drew near, she could hear the sound of revelry, of jolly laughter and pleasant voices; then realizing the loneliness of the road and the fast-gathering gloom around her, she quickened her steps . . . the next moment she saw a stranger coming rapidly towards her. Marguerite did not look up; she was not the least nervous and The Fisherman's Rest was now well within call.

The stranger paused when he saw Marguerite coming quickly towards him, and just as she was about to slip past him, he said very quietly:

"Citizen St Just."

Marguerite uttered a little cry of astonishment. She looked up at the stranger and put out both her hands towards him.

"Chauvelin," she exclaimed.

"At your service, citizen," said the stranger gallantly kissing the tips of her fingers.

Marguerite said nothing for a moment or two, as she looked with obvious delight at the not very attractive figure before her. Chauvelin was then nearer forty than thirty – a clever, shrewd-looking personality, with a curious, foxlike expression in his deep sunken eyes. He was the same stranger who, an hour or two previously, had joined Mr Jellyband in a friendly glass of wine.

Marguerite was pleased to see him. He brought back memories of the happy times in Paris. She did not notice the sarcastic little smile, however, that hovered round the thin lips of Chauvelin.

"But tell me," she said merrily, "what are you doing here in England?"

She had resumed her walk towards the inn, and Chauvelin turned and walked beside her.

"I might ask you the same thing, fair lady," he said, "what about you?"

"Oh," said Marguerite, with a shrug of her shoulders, "I'm just bored, that's all."

"You surprise me," said Chauvelin, glancing at her keenly and taking a pinch of snuff.

"Well, what can you suggest, my little Chauvelin?"

"I can hardly hope to relieve your boredom where Sir Percy Blakeney has so obviously failed."

"Shall we leave Sir Percy out of the question for the present, my dear friend?" said Marguerite. By now they were standing in the porch of the inn and their soft whispers were drowned in the noise which came from the coffee room.

Chauvelin looked at her for a time, observing everything about her. Then he said, "I could make a suggestion but —"

"But what?"

"There *is* Sir Percy."

"What has he to do with it?"

"Quite a good deal, I am afraid. I could offer his wife work."

"Work?"

"Work for France, your country." Chauvelin took a step or two from under the porch, looked quickly and keenly all around him, then, seeing that no one was within earshot, he once more came back close to Marguerite.

"Will you render France a small service, citizeness?" asked Chauvelin earnestly.

"La, man!" said Marguerite, laughing, "how serious you look all of a sudden. What could I possibly do?"

"Have you ever heard of the Scarlet Pimpernel?"

"Heard of the Scarlet Pimpernel? Faith, man, we talk of nothing else!"

"Then you must know," said Chauvelin, in a quiet, hard voice, "that the man who hides his identity under that strange pseudonym is the most bitter enemy of our republic, of France . . . of men like your brother, Armand St Just."

43

"La!" said Marguerite, with a quaint little sigh, "I dare swear he is. France has many bitter enemies these days."

"But you, citizeness, are a daughter of France, and should be ready to help her in a time of deadly peril."

"My brother Armand devotes his life to France," she retorted proudly; "as for me, I can do nothing here in England."

"Listen, citizen, I have been sent over here by the Republican Government as its representative. I present my credentials to your Prime Minister, Mr Pitt, tomorrow. One of my duties here is to find out all about this League of the Scarlet Pimpernel. They are pledged to help our cursed aristocrats – traitors to their country and enemies of the people – to escape from the just punishment they deserve. You know as well as I do that once they are over here, these traitors to France try to arouse public feeling against our Republic and would gladly help any enemy bold enough to attack France. Within this last month, many of these people, some only suspected of treason, others actually condemned by the Tribunal of Public Safety, have succeeded in crossing the Channel. Their escape was organized by the League of the Scarlet Pimpernel headed by a leader who is so clever that none of us can find out who he is. If I can find him, I can find the rest of the gang. Help me, citizen," urged Chauvelin. "Find him for France."

Marguerite had not said a word. She was republican in sympathy and had no love for haughty French aristocrats like the Comtesse de Tournay de Basserive, but her soul recoiled in horror at the Reign of Terror which was taking place in France and she feared that her brother Armand, moderate Republican as he was, might one day become a victim of the guillotine.

When first she heard of this band of young Englishmen, who, for sheer love of their fellows, dragged women and children, old and young men, from a horrible death, her heart had glowed with pride for them, at their courage and the terrible risks they took and she wished she knew their leader. Ah! There was a man she might have loved, had he come her way. Well, she had a duty to the man she *had* married and had sworn her faith and loyalty to him. Her choice was clear.

"You go everywhere," whispered Chauvelin. "You are a leader in society. You see everything, you *hear* everything."

"What you propose is horrible, Chauvelin," said Marguerite, drawing away from him as from some unpleasant insect. "Whoever the Scarlet Pimpernel may be, he is brave and noble, and never – do you hear me? – never would I lend a hand to such villainy. I refuse to do any dirty work for you or for France. You have other means at your disposal; you must use them, my friend."

And without another look at Chauvelin, Marguerite Blakeney turned her back on him and walked straight into the inn.

"That is not your last word, citizen," said Chauvelin, as a flood of light from the passage lit up her elegant, richly clad figure. "We meet in London, I hope."

"We meet in London," she said, speaking over her shoulder at him, "but that is my last word."

She threw open the coffee-room door and disappeared from his view, but he remained under the porch for a moment or two, taking a pinch of snuff. He had received a rebuke and a snub, but his shrewd foxlike face looked neither ashamed nor disappointed; on the contrary, a curious smile, half sarcastic and wholly satisfied, played round the corners of his thin lips.

CHAPTER 9

The Outrage

A beautiful starlit night had followed the day of incessant rain; a cool, balmy late summer's night with a suggestion of moisture and scent of wet earth and dripping leaves.

The magnificent coach, drawn by four of the finest thoroughbreds in England, had driven off along the London road with Sir Percy Blakeney on the box, holding the reins in his slender hands, and beside him Lady Blakeney wrapped in costly furs.

At The Fisherman's Rest Mr Jellyband was going the rounds, putting out the lights. His bar customers had all gone, but upstairs in the snug little bedrooms Mr Jellyband had quite a few important guests: the Comtesse de Tournay, with Suzanne, and the young Vicomte, and there were two more bedrooms ready for Sir Andrew Ffoulkes and Lord Anthony Dewhurst if they should decide to stay the night.

For the moment these two young gallants were sitting comfortably in the coffee room before the huge log fire, which, in spite of the mildness of the evening had been allowed to burn merrily.

"I say, Jelly, has everyone gone?" asked Lord Tony, as the worthy landlord still busied himself clearing away glasses and mugs.

"Everyone, as you can see, my lord."

"And all your servants gone to bed?"

"All except the boy on duty in the bar, and," added Mr Jellyband with a laugh, "I expect he'll be asleep afore long, the rascal."

"Then we can talk here for half an hour without being disturbed?"

"At your service, my lord ... I'll leave your candles on the dresser ... and your rooms are quite ready. I sleep at the top of the house myself, but if your lordship needs anything, just call loudly and I dare say I shall hear."

"All right, Jelly ... and ... I say, put the lamp out – the fire will give us all the light we need – and we don't want to attract the passer-by."

"All right, my lord." Mr Jellyband turned out the quaint old lamp that hung from the raftered ceiling and blew out the candles.

"Let's have a bottle of wine, Jelly," suggested Sir Andrew.

"All right, sir!"

Jellyband went off to fetch the wine. The room now was quite dark except for the light given out by the blazing logs on the fire.

"Is that all, gentlemen?" asked Jellyband, as he returned with a bottle of wine and a couple of glasses, which he placed on the table.

"Thanks, Jelly," said Lord Tony.

"Good night, my lord. Good night, sir."

"Good night, Jelly."

The two young men listened, while the heavy tread of Mr Jellyband was heard echoing along the passage and staircase. Presently even that sound died out, and the whole of The Fisherman's Rest seemed wrapped in sleep, except for the two young men drinking in silence beside the hearth.

For a while no sound was heard, even in the coffee room, save the ticking of the old grandfather clock and the crackling of the burning wood.

"All right again this time, Ffoulkes?" asked Lord Tony at last.

Sir Andrew had been dreaming evidently, gazing into the fire and perhaps seeing there a pretty little face, with

47

large brown eyes and masses of dark curls around a childish forehead.

"Yes," he said thoughtfully, "all right."

"No hitch?"

"None."

Lord Anthony laughed pleasantly as he poured himself out another glass of wine.

"I need not ask, I suppose, whether you found the journey pleasant this time?"

"No, my friend, you need not ask," replied Sir Andrew, smiling. "It was all right."

"Then, here's to her very good health," said Lord Tony, "Mademoiselle Suzanne is a bonnie lass." He drained his glass to the last drop and joined his friend by the fire. The two young men drew their chairs closer together, and, though they were alone, their voices sank to a whisper.

"I saw the Scarlet Pimpernel alone for a few moments in Calais," said Sir Andrew, "a day or two ago. He crossed over to England two days before we did. He had brought the party all the way from Paris dressed as an old market woman and driving a covered cart until they were safely out of the city. The Comtesse de Tournay, Mademoiselle Suzanne and the Vicomte lay concealed among the turnips and cabbages but never suspected who their driver was. He drove them right through a line of soldiery and a yelling mob who were shouting 'Down with the aristos' and he himself shouted louder than anybody." Sir Andrew's eyes glowed with enthusiasm for his beloved leader. "He wants you and Hastings to meet him at Calais," he said quietly, "on the 2nd of next month. Let me see, that will be next Tuesday."

"Yes."

"It is, of course, the Comte de Tournay himself, this time . . . He is under sentence of death and it will be rare sport to get *him* out of France, and you will have a narrow escape, if you get through at all. St Just has gone to meet him. No one suspects St Just as yet, but it will be a tough job. I hope I may yet have orders to be in the rescue party."

"Have you any special instructions for me?"

"Yes, I have. It seems that the French Republican Government have sent a special agent to England. His name is Chauvelin. He is said to be terribly bitter against our league, and determined to discover who our leader is, so that he may have him kidnapped the next time he attempts to set foot in France. This man has brought a whole army of spies with him, and until the chief has found out who they are, he thinks that we should meet as little as possible on the business of the league, and on no account should we talk to each other in public places for a time. When he wants to speak to us, he will find some way of letting us know."

The two young men were both bending over the fire, for the blaze had died down, and only a red glow from the dying embers cast its light on a narrow semicircle in front of the hearth. The rest of the room lay buried in complete gloom. Sir Andrew had produced a pocketbook and drawn from it a paper which he unfolded and together they tried to read it by the dim red firelight. They did not hear a figure which emerged from under one of the benches and with snakelike, noiseless movements crept closer to the two young men, not breathing, only gliding along the floor, in the inky blackness of the room.

"You are to read these instructions and commit them to memory," said Sir Andrew, "then destroy them."

He was about to replace his pocketbook when a tiny slip of paper fluttered from it, and fell on the floor. Lord Anthony stooped and picked it up.

"What's that?" he asked.

"I don't know," replied Sir Andrew.

"It dropped out of your pocket just now. It certainly did not seem to be with the other paper."

"Strange! I wonder when it got there? It is from the chief," he added, glancing at the paper.

Both stooped to try and decipher this last tiny scrap of paper on which a few words had been hastily scrawled, when suddenly a slight noise attracted their attention, which seemed to come from the passage beyond.

"What's that?" they said together. Lord Anthony crossed the room towards the door, which he threw open quickly and suddenly, at that very moment, he received a stunning blow between the eyes, which threw him back violently into the room. At the same time the crouching snakelike figure in the gloom had jumped up and hurled itself from behind upon the unsuspecting Sir Andrew, knocking him to the ground.

All this occurred within the short space of two or three seconds, and before either Lord Anthony or Sir Andrew had time or chance to utter a cry or make a struggle, they were seized by two men, a muffler was quickly tied round the mouth of each, and they were tied to one another back to back, their arms, hands and legs securely fastened.

One man had in the meantime quietly shut the door; he wore a mask and now stood motionless while the others completed their work.

"All safe, citizen!" said one of the men, as he took a final look at the bonds which secured the two young men.

"Good!" replied the man at the door; "now search their pockets and give me all the papers you find."

This was promptly and quietly done. The masked man having taken possession of all the papers, listened for a moment or two if there were any sound within The Fisherman's Rest. All was silent, so he opened the door and pointed down the passage. The four men lifted Sir Andrew and Lord Anthony from the ground, and, as quietly as they had come, they bore the two young gallants out of the inn and along the Dover Road into the gloom beyond.

In the coffee room the masked leader of this daring attempt was quickly glancing through the stolen papers.

"Not a bad day's work on the whole," he muttered, as he

quietly took off his mask, and his pale, foxlike eyes glittered in the red glow of the fire. "Not a bad day's work."

He opened one or two more letters from Sir Andrew Ffoulkes' pocketbook, and noted the tiny scrap of paper which the two young men had only just had time to read, but one letter especially, signed Armand St Just, seemed to give him strange satisfaction.

"Armand St Just is a traitor after all," he murmured. "Now, fair Marguerite Blakeney," he added viciously beneath his clenched teeth, "I think you will help me to find the Scarlet Pimpernel."

CHAPTER 10

In the Opera Box

It was one of the gala nights at Covent Garden Theatre, the first of the summer season in this year of grace 1792.

The house was packed, both in the smart orchestra boxes and the pit, as well as in the cheaper balconies and galleries above. Glück's *Orpheus* was being performed and now the curtain was coming down at the end of the second act to a tumult of applause led by the Prince of Wales from the royal box. The audience seemed as one to breathe a sigh of satisfaction and immediately let loose its hundreds of waggish and frivolous tongues. The Prince of Wales, jovial, round, somewhat coarse and commonplace in appearance moved about from box to box spending a short time with some of his closer friends.

In Lord Grenville's box, a curious interesting personality attracted everyone's attention, a thin small figure, with a shrewd, sarcastic face and deep-set eyes. He was dressed in black and his dark hair was unpowdered. Lord Grenville

– the Foreign Secretary of State paid him marked respect, but was cold in his manner towards him.

In the audience were one or two French royalist refugees. They had sad faces and the women especially paid little heed either to the music or the brilliant audience; no doubt their thoughts were with a husband, brother or son still in peril in France or recently killed by the Revolutionary Government. Among them was the Comtesse de Tournay de Basserive, dressed in deep, heavy black silk with only a white lace kerchief to relieve her appearance of mourning. She sat beside Lady Portarles, who was vainly trying to make her smile with jokes and witty remarks. Behind her, in the box sat little Suzanne and the Vicomte, both silent and somewhat shy among so many strangers. Suzanne had looked round eagerly, hoping to see Sir Andrew, but, not seeing him, she settled herself quietly behind her mother, sat through the music and took no further interest in the audience.

There was a knock on the door at the back of the box and the clever, interesting face of the Secretary of State appeared.

"Come in, Lord Grenville," cried Lady Portarles. "Here is Madame la Comtesse de Tournay, anxious to hear the latest news from France."

"Alas," said the distinguished diplomat, as he shook hands, "it is of the very worst. The massacres continue and the guillotine claims a hundred victims a day."

The Comtesse was leaning back in her chair, pale and tearful.

"Ah, Monsieur," she said in broken English, "it is terrible for me to be sitting here in a theatre, all safe and in peace, while he is in such peril."

"But Madame," said Lord Grenville, "did you not tell me yesterday that the League of the Scarlet Pimpernel had pledged their honour to bring your husband safely across the Channel?"

"Ah yes," replied the Comtesse, "and that is my only hope. I saw Lord Hastings yesterday and he reassured me."

"Lord Grenville," said Lady Portarles, who was somewhat outspoken, "I don't like the look of that French scarecrow you have in your box."

"He is my guest," said Lord Grenville, "and the representative of his government."

"Heavens, man," retorted her ladyship, "you don't call those bloodthirsty ruffians over there a government, do you?"

"I have to receive him," said Lord Grenville guardedly, "he is the representative of a country with which we have diplomatic relations."

"Diplomatic relations be demmed, my lord! That sly little fox over there is nothing but a spy, I'll warrant, and you'll find that he has come to do harm to royalist refugees, to our heroic Scarlet Pimpernel, and to the members of that brave little league."

"I am sure," said the Comtesse, pursing up her thin lips, "that if this Chauvelin wishes to do us harm, he will find a faithful ally in Lady Blakeney."

"Madame," said Lady Portarles, turning a wrathful and resolute face towards the Comtesse, "Lady Blakeney may or may not be in sympathy with those ruffians in France, but she is the leader of fashion in this country; Sir Percy Blakeney has more money than any half-dozen other men put together, he is hand in glove with royalty, and your trying to snub Lady Blakeney, as I hear you did recently, will not harm her, but will make you look a fool. Isn't that so, my lord?"

But what Lord Grenville thought or how the Comtesse responded to this reproof was not known, for the curtain had just risen on the third act of *Orpheus*, and cries of "Silence!" came from every part of the house.

Lord Grenville took a hasty farewell of the ladies and slipped back into his box, where Monsieur Chauvelin had sat all through the interval, with his snuffbox in his hand, and with his keen pale eyes intently fixed upon a box opposite to him, where, with much frou-frou of silken skirts, much laughter and general stir of curiosity among the audience, Marguerite Blakeney had just entered accompanied by her husband. She looked divinely pretty; her wealth of golden, reddish curls, slightly sprinkled with powder, were tied back at the nape of her graceful neck with a gigantic black bow.

Marguerite was passionately fond of music and *Orpheus* charmed her tonight. She was especially happy because she had received the news that the *Day Dream* had returned from Calais and that her brother had safely landed. He had sent a message that he thought of her and would be prudent for her sake.

She became absorbed in the music and hardly noticed when her husband left their box to see his friends. Plenty came to pay court, including the Prince of Wales. When he left, she dismissed the rest, wishing to enjoy the music of Glück alone for a while.

A discreet knock at the door roused her from her enjoyment.

"Come in," she said with some impatience, without turning to look at the intruder.

Chauvelin looked in, saw that she was alone, quietly slipped into the box and the next moment was standing behind Marguerite's chair.

"A word with you, citizen," he said quietly.

Marguerite turned quickly, in alarm, which was not entirely pretended.

"Lud, man! you frightened me," she said, with a forced little laugh. "I am listening to music and have no mind for talking."

"But this is my only opportunity to see you alone," he said and without waiting for permission he drew a chair close behind her – so close that he could whisper in her ear, without disturbing the audience and without being seen, in the dark background of the box.

54

"Faith, man!" said Marguerite impatiently, "you must seek for another opportunity then. I am going to Lord Grenville's ball tonight after the opera. So are you, probably. I'll give you five minutes then."

"Three minutes in the privacy of this box are quite sufficient for me," rejoined Chauvelin placidly, "but I think you would be wise to listen to me, Citizen St Just."

Marguerite shivered in spite of herself. Chauvelin had not raised his voice above a whisper; he was now quietly taking a pinch of snuff, yet there was something in his attitude, something in those pale, foxy eyes which seemed to freeze the blood in her veins.

"Is that a threat, citizen?"

"No, fair lady, only an arrow shot into the air. Your brother Armand St Just is in peril."

He saw her stiffen, though she pretended to be looking at the stage and with her hand she began to beat time nervously against the cushion of the box.

"Well?" she said suddenly, without turning her head.

"Well, citizen?" he returned calmly.

"About my brother?"

"I have news of him for you which, I think will interest you. Let me explain."

Her head was still turned away but he knew that every nerve was strained to hear what he had to say.

"The other day," said Chauvelin, "I asked for your help. France needed it and I thought I could rely on you, but you gave me your answer."

"I gave you my answer," said Marguerite, trying to speak lightly. "Now let us listen to the music, which is entrancing. The audience will get impatient with your talk. Pray come to the point and then be silent."

"I will explain. The day on which I had the honour of meeting you at Dover, and less than an hour after you gave me your final answer, some papers came into my possession. They appeared to be plans for the escape of a batch of French aristocrats, including that traitor de Tournay, organized by that arch-meddler, the Scarlet Pimpernel. I know something of his League, but not enough, and you *must* help me."

Marguerite seemed to have listened to him with marked impatience. She now spoke as if the matter was of no importance.

"Bah, man. Have I not already told you that I have no interest in your schemes or the Scarlet Pimpernel? I would not be listening to you now if you had not spoken of my brother."

"A little patience, I entreat," replied Chauvelin softly. "Two gentlemen, Lord Anthony Dewhurst and Sir Andrew Ffoulkes, were at The Fisherman's Rest at Dover that same night."

"I know. I saw them there."

"They were already known to my spies as members of that accursed League. It was Sir Andrew Ffoulkes who escorted the Comtesse de Tournay and her children across the Channel. When the two young men were alone, my spies forced their way into the coffee room of the inn, gagged them and tied them up, seized their papers, and brought them to me."

In a moment she had guessed the danger. Papers? They could involve Armand. She was struck with terror, but she would not allow this man to see she feared him. She laughed lightly.

"Faith! Your impudence passes belief," she said merrily. "Robbery and violence! In England! In a crowded inn. Your men might have been caught in the act!"

"What if they had? They are Frenchmen trained by me. Had they been caught they would have gone to jail, or even the gallows, without a word rather than reveal our secrets. At any rate, it was well worth the risk."

"Tell me about those papers you have," she said carelessly.

"They give me some information, some names, but I have still not found out the identity of the Scarlet Pimpernel."

"Well then, why did you speak to me about my brother?"

"I am coming to him now, citizen. Among the papers there was a letter to Sir Andrew Ffoulkes from your brother St Just. This letter shows him to be not only in sympathy with the enemies of France, but actually a helper, if not a member, of the League of the Scarlet Pimpernel."

The blow had been struck at last and Marguerite knew that he spoke the truth. She knew it as if she had seen the letter with her own eyes and Chauvelin would hold it for purposes of his own until it suited him to destroy it or to make use of it against Armand. She threw her head back and laughed as if she did not believe him.

"Let me make one point clear," said Chauvelin calmly. "Your brother is mixed up in this beyond the slightest hope of pardon."

Inside the orchestra box all was silent for a moment or two. Marguerite sat without moving, thinking hard. At last she said quite seriously, "Chauvelin, my friend, shall we try to understand one another? You are very anxious to find out who the Scarlet Pimpernel is and you are trying to force me to do some spying work for you in exchange for my brother's safety. That is it, isn't it?"

"You are using two very ugly words, fair lady," protested Chauvelin. "There can be no question of force, and the service which I ask of you, in the name of France, could never be called by the shocking name of spying."

"At any rate, that is what it is called over here," she said without emotion. "That is your intention, is it not?"

"My intention is, that you yourself win a free pardon for Armand St Just by doing me a small service."

"What is it?"

"Only watch for me tonight," he said eagerly. "Listen: among the papers which were found on Sir Andrew Ffoulkes there was a tiny note. Look," he added, taking a tiny scrap of paper from his pocketbook and handing it to her.

It was the same scrap of paper which, four days before, the two young men were reading when they were attacked by Chauvelin's men. Marguerite took it and stooped to read it. There were only two lines, written in a disguised handwriting; she read them half aloud:

"Remember we must not meet more often than is strictly necessary. You have your orders for the 2nd. If you wish to speak to me again, I shall be at G's ball." In the corner of the note was a little red flower emblem.

"The Scarlet Pimpernel!" cried Marguerite, "and G stands for Lord Grenville. He will be at my Lord Grenville's ball tonight."

"That is what I think too," said Chauvelin. "We released Lord Anthony and Sir Andrew this morning. They will have a great deal now to say to their chief and I think we can safely conclude that they can ride to London by tonight. If they are watched at the ball, they may lead us to their master. You can help me. Find out who the Scarlet Pimpernel is, and I will pledge the word of France that your brother shall be safe."

Chauvelin meant what he said. Marguerite knew he would stop at nothing and she played for time.

"If I promise to help you in this matter, Chauvelin," she said pleasantly, "will you give me that letter written by my brother?"

"If you help me tonight, I will give you that letter tomorrow."

"I may be powerless to help you," she pleaded, "even if I wanted to."

"That would be terrible indeed," he said quietly, "both for you and for St Just."

Marguerite shuddered. She felt lonely and frightened for Armand's sake and longed to seek comfort and advice from someone who could help her. Sir Percy Blakeney had loved her once; he was her husband; why should she stand alone through this terrible ordeal? He was not clever but he was strong. She was sure he could help.

Chauvelin was paying no further attention to her. He

appeared to be listening to the music and was beating time with his sharp ferretlike head.

A soft tap at the door roused Marguerite from her thoughts. It was Percy Blakeney, tall, sleepy, good-humoured, and wearing that half-shy, half-silly smile, which just now seemed to irritate her every nerve.

"Your chair is outside, m'dear," he said with his most exasperating drawl, "I suppose you will want to go to that demmed ball. Excuse me – er – Monsieur Chauvelin – I had not observed you."

He extended two slender, white fingers towards Chauvelin, who had risen when Sir Percy entered the box.

"Are you coming, m'dear?"

Cries of "Hush!" came from different parts of the house.

"Demmed impudence," commented Sir Percy with a good-natured smile.

Marguerite sighed impatiently. Her last hope seemed to have vanished away. She wrapped her cloak round her and, without looking at her husband, said "I am ready to go," and took his arm. At the door of the box she turned and looked straight at Chauvelin, who, with his hat under his arm, and a curious smile round his thin lips, was preparing to follow them.

"We shall meet at Lord Grenville's ball, Chauvelin," said Marguerite.

As they left Chauvelin bowed, took a pinch of snuff and rubbed his thin, bony hands contentedly together.

CHAPTER 11

Lord Grenville's Ball

Lord Grenville's ball was the most brilliant function of the year and everybody who was anybody tried to be in London for it, so that they could attend and shine to the best of his or her ability.

His Royal Highness the Prince of Wales had promised to be present. He was coming on from the opera. Lord Grenville himself had listened to the first two acts of *Orpheus*, before preparing to receive his guests. At ten o'clock – an unusually late hour in those days – the grand rooms of the Foreign Office, exquisitely decorated with exotic palms and flowers, were filled to overflowing. One room had been set apart for dancing, and the dainty strains of the minuet mingled with the chatter and merry laughter of the guests.

In the small chamber, facing the top of the fine stairway, the distinguished host stood ready to receive his guests and near him, leaning against a small table, stood Monsieur Chauvelin in his neat, black suit casting his eye over the brilliant throng of people. He noticed that Sir Percy and Lady Blakeney had not yet arrived, and his keen, pale eyes glanced quickly towards the door every time a newcomer appeared.

Chauvelin was there as the official representative of France and, as such, had been entertained more than once by Lord Grenville and been received by Mr Pitt, the Prime Minister, but because of the Reign of Terror on the other side of the Channel, Society people ignored him altogether; the women openly turned their backs on him; the men who held no official position refused to shake his hand.

Suddenly there was a great stir on the handsome staircase, all conversation stopped for a moment as the major-domo's voice outside announced –

"His Royal Highness, the Prince of Wales, Sir Percy and Lady Blakeney."

Lord Grenville went quickly to the door to receive his exalted guest.

The Prince of Wales, dressed in a magnificent court suit of salmon-coloured velvet richly embroidered with gold, entered with Marguerite Blakeney on his arm; and on his left came Sir Percy, in gorgeous, shimmering cream satin, his fair hair free from powder, and priceless lace at his neck and wrists.

After a few words of respectful greeting, Lord Grenville said to his royal guest –

"Will your Royal Highness permit me to introduce Monsieur Chauvelin, the representative of the French Government?"

Chauvelin stepped forward and bowed very low, while the Prince responded with a curt nod of the head.

"Monsieur," said His Royal Highness coldly, "we will try to forget the Government that sent you, and look upon you merely as our guest – a private gentleman from France. As such you are welcome, Monsieur."

"Monseigneur," rejoined Chauvelin, bowing once again.

"Madame," he added, bowing ceremoniously before Marguerite.

"Ah! my little Chauvelin!" she said and extended her tiny hand to him. "Monsieur and I are old friends, your Royal Highness."

"Ah, then," said the Prince, this time very graciously, "you are doubly welcome, Monsieur."

The Comtesse de Tournay de Basserive was the next to be presented and she in turn presented her son, the Vicomte.

"I am happy to know you, Monsieur le Vicomte," said the Prince. "I knew your father well when he was ambassador in London."

"Ah, Monseigneur!" replied the Vicomte. "I was a little boy then . . . and now I owe the honour of this meeting to our protector, the Scarlet Pimpernel."

"Hush!" said the Prince earnestly and quickly, glancing at Chauvelin.

"Pray do not check this gentleman's display of gratitude, Monsieur," said the Frenchman. "The name of that interesting red flower the Scarlet Pimpernel is well known to me – and to France."

The Prince looked at him keenly for a moment or two.

"Then, Monsieur," he said, "perhaps you know more about our national hero than we do ourselves. Perhaps you know who he is."

"Ah, Monseigneur," said Chauvelin, "rumour has it in France that your Royal Highness could – if he would – give the truest account of that mysterious little flower."

Marguerite, who had exchanged cold, formal curtsies with the Comtesse, was still standing near. Chauvelin looked quickly and keenly at her as he spoke, but she betrayed no emotion, and her eyes met his quite fearlessly.

"My lips are sealed," said the Prince. "We know not if he be tall or short, fair or dark, handsome or ugly; but we know that the Scarlet Pimpernel is the bravest gentleman in all the

62

world, and we all feel a little proud when we remember that he is an Englishman."

"Ah, Monsieur Chauvelin," added Marguerite, looking almost with defiance across at the placid, sphinxlike face of the Frenchman, "His Royal Highness should add that we ladies think of him as a hero of old . . . we worship him . . . we wear his badge . . . we tremble for him when he is in danger, and rejoice with him in the hour of his victory."

Chauvelin did no more than bow placidly both to the Prince and to Marguerite; he felt that both speeches were intended – each in their way – to convey contempt or defiance. The pleasure-loving idle Prince he despised; the beautiful woman who in her golden hair wore a spray of small red flowers composed of rubies and diamonds – her he held in the hollow of his hand: he could afford to remain silent and await events.

A long, jolly, silly laugh broke the sudden silence which had fallen over everyone.

"And we poor husbands," drawled Sir Percy, "we have to stand by while they worship a demmed shadow."

Everyone laughed – the Prince more loudly than anyone, the group broke up and they dispersed into the adjoining rooms.

CHAPTER 12

The Scrap of Paper

Marguerite suffered intensely and most especially because she saw that it would be useless to expect help from her husband in the terrible situation in which she found herself. There he stood, the one who should have been the moral support, the cool-headed adviser, surrounded by a crowd of brainless young dandies, who were even now repeating from mouth to mouth, and with every sign of the keenest enjoyment, a little rhyme which he had just made up.

"All done in the tying of a cravat," Sir Percy had declared to his group of admirers.

> We seek him here, we seek him there,
> Those Frenchies seek him everywhere.
> Is he in heaven? – Is he in hell?
> That demmed elusive Pimpernel.

Presently Sir Percy was claimed by the Prince, who took him off to the card tables, and Marguerite was left surrounded by her usual crowd of admirers. She was apparently happy and sparkling but all she could really think of was that she could expect no mercy from Chauvelin. He had set a price upon Armand's head, and left it to her to pay or not, as she chose.

Later on in the evening she caught sight of Sir Andrew Ffoulkes and Lord Anthony Dewhurst, who seemingly had just arrived. She noticed at once that Sir Andrew immediately made for little Suzanne de Tournay and that the two young people went off to a seat by the window where they carried on a long conversation, which seemed very earnest and very enjoyable to both of them.

Both young men looked a little haggard and anxious, but they were perfectly dressed and gave no sign of the terrible catastrophe which they must have felt hovering round them and their chief.

Marguerite knew that the League of the Scarlet Pimpernel had no intention of giving up their plan to rescue the Comte de Tournay within the next few days. Suzanne had told her this and a burning curiosity seized her to know who the leader was. He must be at the ball, of course, somewhere, since Sir Andrew Ffoulkes and Lord Anthony Dewhurst were here evidently expecting to meet their chief – and perhaps to get further orders from him. Marguerite looked around her and wondered which of the guests was concealing the power, the energy, the cunning which had imposed its will and its leadership upon a number of high-born English gentlemen, among whom, so she had heard it said was His Royal Highness himself.

Could it be Sir Andrew Ffoulkes? Surely not, with his gentle blue eyes, which were looking so tenderly and longingly after Suzanne, who was being led away from him by her stern mother. Marguerite watched him across the room, and he finally turned away with a sigh, and seemed to stand, aimless and lonely, now that Suzanne's dainty little figure had disappeared in the crowd.

She watched him as he strolled towards the doorway, which led to a small boudoir beyond, then paused and leaned against the framework of it, looking still anxiously all around him.

Marguerite made some excuse to an admirer who had been hovering attentively at her side and moved towards the doorway against which Sir Andrew was leaning. Why she did this she could not have said, except that instinct made her do so.

Suddenly she stopped: her very heart seemed to stand still, her eyes, large and excited, flashed for a moment towards that doorway, then as quickly were turned away again. Sir Andrew was still by the door, but Marguerite had distinctly seen that Lord Hastings – a friend of her husband's and one of the Prince's set – had, as he quickly brushed past him, slipped something into his hand.

Casually Marguerite continued her walk across the room towards the doorway through which Sir Andrew had now disappeared. She forgot everything except that her beloved brother stood in peril of his life and that there, not twenty feet away from her, in the small boudoir, in the very hands of Sir Andrew Ffoulkes, might be the talisman which would save Armand's life.

She slipped quietly through the doorway of the boudoir. Sir Andrew was alone there standing with his back to her and close to a table upon which stood a massive silver candelabra. A slip of paper was in his hand and he was reading its contents. Marguerite came silently up behind him . . . At that moment he looked round and saw her; she uttered a groan, passed her hand across her forehead, and murmured faintly –

"The heat in the room was terrible. I think I am going to faint."

She tottered almost as if she would fall, and Sir Andrew, quickly recovering himself, and crumpling in his hand the tiny note he had been reading, was only, apparently, just in time to catch her.

"You are ill, Lady Blakeney?" he asked with much concern. "Let me help you to this chair." She sank into the chair which was close to the table, and throwing back her head, closed her eyes.

For one moment there was silence in the little boudoir. Beyond, from the brilliant ballroom, the sweet notes of the gavotte, the frou-frou of rich dresses, the talk and laughter of a large and merry crowd, came as a strange, weird accompaniment to the drama which was taking place here.

Sir Andrew had not uttered another word, but Marguerite became aware of an extra sense. She could not see, for her eyes were closed; she could not hear, for the noise from the ballroom drowned the soft rustle of that important scrap of paper; nevertheless she knew – as if she had both seen and heard – that Sir Andrew was even now holding the paper to the flame of one of the candles.

At the exact moment that it began to catch fire, she opened her eyes, raised her hand, and with two dainty fingers, had taken the burning scrap of paper from the young man's hand. Then she blew out the flame, and held the paper to her nostrils.

"How thoughtful of you, Sir Andrew," she cried, "surely 'twas your grandmother who taught you that the smell of burnt paper was a remedy for giddiness."

She sighed with satisfaction, holding the paper tightly between her jewelled fingers. Sir Andrew was staring at her, racking his brains as to the quickest method he could employ to get that bit of paper out of that beautiful woman's hand. Alarming thoughts rushed through his mind: he suddenly remembered her nationality, and, worst of all, recollected that horrible tale about the Marquis de St Cyr and his family, which in England no one had believed, for the sake of her husband, Sir Percy, as well as for her own. Pulling himself together he said, "Lady Blakeney, that note is mine. Please give it back to me." Not caring if his action would be thought rude, he made a bold dash for the note, but Marguerite's thoughts flew quicker than his own; her actions were swifter and more sure. She was tall and strong, she took a quick step backwards and knocked over the small Sheraton table which was already top-heavy, and which fell with a crash, together with the massive candelabra upon it.

She gave a quick cry of alarm.

"The candles, Sir Andrew – quick!"

There was not much damage done; one or two of the candles had blown out as the candelabra fell; others had merely sent some grease upon the valuable carpet; one had burnt the paper shade over it. Sir Andrew quickly put out the flames and replaced the candelabra upon the table; but this had taken a few seconds for him to do, and those seconds had been all that Marguerite needed to cast a quick glance at the paper and to note its contents – a dozen words in the same handwriting she had seen before and bearing the same device – a star-shaped flower drawn in red ink. She let the paper flutter to the ground and Sir Andrew did not realize that she had seen it. Eagerly he picked it up looking very relieved as his fingers closed tightly over it. Twisting it up, he held it to the flame of the candle which had remained alight, not noticing the strange smile on the face of his companion; perhaps, had he done so, the look of relief would have faded from his face. He watched the fateful note as it curled under the flame. Soon the last fragment fell on the floor, and he placed his heel upon the ashes.

"And now, Sir Andrew," said Marguerite Blakeney with a winning smile, "will you honour me by asking me to dance the minuet?"

CHAPTER 13

Either – or?

The few words which Marguerite Blakeney had managed to read on the half-scorched piece of paper seemed to her the words of fate. "Start myself tomorrow . . ." She had read this quite clearly, then came a smudge caused by the smoke of the candle, but, right at the bottom, she had read another sentence: "If you wish to speak to me again, I shall be in the supper room at one o'clock precisely." The paper was signed with the tiny red star-shaped flower – the Scarlet Pimpernel.

It was now close on eleven and Marguerite was dancing a minuet with Sir Andrew Ffoulkes. In two hours she would have to make up her mind whether to keep the knowledge she had gained from the scrap of paper to herself and leave her brother to his fate, or whether she would wilfully betray a brave man, whose life was devoted to saving his fellow men, a man who was noble, generous and above all unsuspecting. It seemed a horrible thing to do, but then her beloved brother was facing a horrible death. He trusted her and now, when she could save him, she hesitated.

These thoughts ran round and round her head while she was dancing, but nobody who saw her sunny smile would have realized it.

When the minuet was over, she asked Sir Andrew to

take her into the next room. He seemed quite reassured.

"I have promised to go down to supper with His Royal Highness. I am so sorry about the accident with the candles."

In the room beyond His Royal Highness was waiting for her.

"Madame, supper awaits us," said the Prince, offering his arm to Marguerite.

"Has your Highness been fortunate at the card tables?" asked Marguerite.

"No Madame, your husband has the most confounded luck, but this life would be a dreary desert without his jokes and your smiles."

CHAPTER 14

One o'clock precisely!

During supper Marguerite appeared in her most brilliant mood and the Prince had laughed till the tears poured down his cheeks at some of Sir Percy's jokes.

The clock was ticking mercilessly on. It was long past midnight, and even the Prince of Wales was thinking of leaving the supper table. Within the next half-hour the fates of two brave men would be pitted against one another – the dearly loved brother and he, the unknown hero. Marguerite had avoided Chauvelin. She knew his keen, foxlike eyes would terrify her and tip the balance in favour of Armand. While she did not see him, she had a vague, undefined hope that something might happen to take away this terrible burden from her young, weak shoulders.

After supper, dancing was resumed and His Royal Highness left. Marguerite declined all offers to dance and slipped away from her admirers to the tiny boudoir which was still the most deserted of all the rooms. She knew that Chauvelin must be lying in wait for her somewhere and she had to be alone and think.

Before she had been there five minutes, Chauvelin, who must have been watching her, slipped into the room, and stood by her side.

"You have news for me?" he said.

An icy mantle seemed to have suddenly settled round Marguerite's shoulders; though her cheeks glowed with fire, she felt chilled and numbed.

"Nothing of importance," she said. "I found Sir Andrew Ffoulkes in the very act of burning a paper at one of these candles, in this very room. That paper I succeeded in holding between my fingers for the space of two minutes (never mind how I managed it), and I had ten seconds to look at it."

"Time enough to learn its contents?" asked Chauvelin quietly.

"Yes, in the corner of the paper there was the device of a small, red, star-shaped flower. Above it I read two lines, everything else was scorched and blackened by the flame."

Her throat seemed suddenly to have contracted. For an instant she felt that she could not speak the words which might send a brave man to his death.

"It is lucky that the whole paper was not burned," added Chauvelin, "for that might have turned out badly for Armand St Just. What were the two lines, citizen?"

"One was, 'I start myself tomorrow,'" she said quietly, "the other – 'if you wish to speak to me, I shall be in the supper room at one o'clock precisely.'"

Chauvelin looked up at the clock just above the mantelpiece.

"Then I have plenty of time," he said.

"What are you going to do?"

"Nothing for the present. After that it depends."

"Depends on what?"

"On whom I shall see in the supper room at one o'clock precisely."

"You will see the Scarlet Pimpernel, of course. But you do not know him."

"No. But I shall soon."

"Sir Andrew will have warned him."

"I think not. I have been watching him. At supper he had ladies on either side. The rest of the time he was dancing or talking with Mademoiselle de Tournay. I think I may safely expect to find the person I seek in the supper room."

"There may be more than one."

"Whoever is there, as the clock strikes one, will be shadowed by one or more of my men. Whether there are one, two or even three men leaving for France tomorrow, *one* of them will be the Scarlet Pimpernel."

"And what will *you* do?"

"I also will leave for France tomorrow. In the papers which we took from Sir Andrew Ffoulkes we found the name of an inn which I know well, called Le Chat Gris and mention of a lonely place somewhere on the coast – the Père Blanchard's Hut, and this place I must try to find. The Comte de Tournay is there waiting to be rescued. There I hope to capture that mysterious and elusive Pimpernel."

"And Armand?" she pleaded.

"Have I ever broken my word? I promise you that the day the Scarlet Pimpernel and I start for France, I will send that unwise letter of his to you by special courier. More than that, I pledge you the word of France that the day I lay hands on that meddlesome Englishman, Armand St Just will be here in England, safe with his charming sister."

And with a deep and elaborate bow and a look at the clock, Chauvelin glided out of the room.

Marguerite lay back in her chair, exhausted and miserable, while Chauvelin made his way to the now deserted supper room. All was silent there and the room had a for-saken appearance, the table littered with half-empty glasses and unfolded napkins and the chairs all over the place. Chauvelin smiled and rubbed his thin hands together. Then he settled down to wait. He thought he was alone, but after a few minutes, he became aware that one of Lord Grenville's guests was there enjoying a quiet sleep, away from the noise of the dancing above. He looked round and there in a corner of the sofa, in the dark angle of the room, his mouth open, his eyes shut, the sweet sounds of peaceful slumbers pro-ceeding from his nostrils, reclined the gorgeously dressed long-limbed husband of the cleverest woman in Europe, Marguerite Blakeney. Evidently the sleeper, deep in dreamless sleep, would not interfere with Chauvelin's trap for catching that cunning Scarlet Pimpernel. Again he rubbed his hands together, and, following the example of Sir Percy Blakeney, he too stretched himself out in the corner of another sofa, shut his eyes, opened his mouth, gave forth sounds of peaceful breathing, and . . . waited!

CHAPTER 15

Doubt

Marguerite waited a full hour in the boudoir. She was in an agony of mind, wondering what was happening in the supper room. Lord Grenville himself came at length to tell her that her coach was ready and that Sir Percy was waiting for her, reins in hand.

At the top of the stairs, just after she had taken leave of her host and some of his other guests, she suddenly saw Chauvelin; he was coming up the stairs slowly, rubbing his hands softly together. There was a curious look on his face, partly amused and wholly puzzled and he looked keenly at Marguerite.

"Monsieur Chauvelin," she said, as he stopped at the top of the stairs and bowed to her, "my coach is outside; may I claim your arm?"

As gallant as ever, he offered her his arm and led her downstairs.

"Chauvelin," she said, "I must know what has happened."

"Nothing has happened, dear lady. In the supper room quiet and peace reigned supreme and when one o'clock came, I was asleep in the corner of one sofa and Sir Percy Blakeney was asleep in another."

"Nobody came into the room at all?"

"Nobody."

"Then we have failed?"

"Yes, we have failed – perhaps."

"But what about Armand?"

"Ah! Armand St Just's chances hang on a thread. Pray heaven that thread may not snap."

"Chauvelin, I did try to help you."

"I remember my promise," he said quietly; "the day that the Scarlet Pimpernel and I meet on French soil, St Just will be safe with his charming sister."

"Which means that a brave man's blood will be on my hands," she said, with a shudder.

"His blood or that of your brother. Surely at the present moment you must hope as I do, that the Scarlet Pimpernel will start for Calais today."

"I am only conscious of one hope, citizen."

"And what is that, citizen?"

"That Satan, your master will have need of you, elsewhere, before the sun rises today." And with that, she left him.

CHAPTER 16

Richmond

A few minutes later she was sitting, wrapped in costly furs, near Sir Percy Blakeney on the box-seat of his magnificent coach, and the four splendid bays had thundered down the quiet street.

The night was warm in spite of the gentle breeze which fanned Marguerite's burning cheeks.

Soon London houses were left behind, and rattling over old Hammersmith Bridge, Sir Percy was driving his bays rapidly towards Richmond.

The river wound in and out in its pretty delicate curves, looking like a silver serpent beneath the glittering rays of the moon.

Long shadows from overhanging trees from time to time spread dark mantles right across the road. The bays were rushing along at breakneck speed, held but slightly back by Sir Percy's strong hands.

These nightly drives after balls and suppers in London

74

were a delight to Marguerite and she appreciated her husband taking her home every night, to their beautiful home by the river, instead of living in a stuffy London house. Sir Percy loved driving his spirited horses along the lonely, moonlit roads, and she loved to sit on the box-seat, with the soft air of an English late summer's night fanning her face, after the hot atmosphere of a ball or supper party. The drive was not a long one – less than an hour, sometimes, when the bays were very fresh, and Sir Percy gave them full rein.

Tonight he seemed to have a very devil in his fingers, and the coach seemed to fly along the road, beside the river. As usual, he did not speak to her, but stared straight in front of him, the reins seeming to lie quite loosely in his slender, white hands. Marguerite looked at him once or twice. His face in the moonlight was serious and determined and Marguerite remembered with an aching heart those happy days of courtship, before he had become the lazy nincompoop, the pleasure-loving fop, whose life seemed spent in cards and supper rooms.

As she felt her husband's strong arm beside her, Marguerite felt how much he would dislike and despise her, if he knew of this night's work. For the sake of her brother, she had done something which she knew to be wrong.

Buried in her thoughts, Marguerite had found this hour in the breezy summer night all too brief; and it was with a feeling of keen disappointment that she suddenly realized that the horses had turned into the massive gates of her beautiful English home.

With his sure touch, Sir Percy had brought the four bays to a standstill immediately in front of the fine Elizabethan entrance hall. In spite of the lateness of the hour, an army of grooms seemed to have emerged from the very ground, as the coach had thundered up and were standing respectfully round.

Sir Percy stepped down quickly, then helped Marguerite to alight. She lingered outside for a moment, while he gave orders to one of his men. She skirted the house, and stepped on to the lawn, looking out dreamily into the silvery landscape. She could faintly hear the ripple of the river and the occasional soft and ghostlike fall of a dead leaf from a tree. Marguerite sighed. Never had she felt so pitiably lonely, so bitterly in need of comfort and of sympathy. With another sigh she turned away from the river towards the house, wondering if she would ever find peace of mind again.

Suddenly, before she reached the terrace, she heard a firm step upon the crisp gravel, and the next moment her husband's figure emerged out of the shadow. He was wandering now along the lawn, towards the river and seemed not to have noticed her, for after a moment's pause he turned back towards the house, and walked straight up to the terrace.

"Sir Percy!"

"At your service, Madame!"

He looked her straight in the eyes in that lazy way which had become second nature to him. She returned his gaze for a moment, then her eyes softened as she came up quite close to him, to the foot of the terrace steps.

She looked divinely pretty as she stood there in the moonlight, with the fur coat sliding off her beautiful shoulders, the gold embroidery on her dress shimmering around her, her blue eyes gazing up at him.

He stood for a moment, rigid and still, but for the clenching of his hand against the stone balustrade of the terrace.

"How can I serve you, Madame?"

"Sir Percy, cannot we return to the love we shared at the time of our marriage?"

"Twenty-four hours after that marriage, Madame, the Marquis de St Cyr and all his family perished on the guillotine, and the popular rumour reached me that it was the wife of Sir Percy Blakeney who helped to send them there."

"But I myself told you the truth about that."

"Not until after it had been recounted to me by strangers, with all its horrible details."

"And you believed them. You thought I meant to deceive you, that I should have told you about it before we were married. Had you listened to me you would have known that up to the very morning St Cyr went to the guillotine, I was using all the influence I possessed to save him and his family. I was tricked by men who knew how to play upon my love for my brother, and my desire for revenge on the man who had treated him so brutally."

Marguerite's voice became choked with tears and she looked appealingly at him as if he were her judge.

Sir Percy did not answer. The dim grey light of early dawn seemed to make his tall form taller and more rigid. The lazy, good-natured face looked strangely altered. A curious look of intense passion seemed to glow from his eyes, his mouth was tightly closed as if he were holding himself in check.

In that moment, she knew that he loved her. His passion might be sleeping, but it was there, as strong, as intense, as overwhelming, as when first her lips met his in one long, maddening kiss.

"Listen to the tale, Sir Percy," she said and her voice now was low, sweet, infinitely tender. "Armand was all in all to me! We had no parents and brought one another up. One day the Marquis de St Cyr had my brother thrashed by his servants because he, a man of the people, had dared to love the daughter of a nobleman. His suffering became mine too and when an opportunity occurred to take my revenge, I took it.

"But I only thought to bring that proud marquis to trouble and humiliation. He plotted with Austria against his own country. I found this out by chance and spoke of it, but I did not know – how could I guess? – they trapped me into it, and when I realized what I had done, it was too late."

"I seem to remember," said Sir Percy, "that when I asked

you about the rumours, you refused to answer – you refused me any explanation."

"I wished to test your love for me, and it did not bear the test."

"And for me to prove my love, you demanded that I should sacrifice my honour. I did not *ask* for an explanation – I *waited* for one, not doubting you – only hoping. Had you spoken but one word, I would have accepted your explanation and believed it. But you left me without a word, apart from telling me what you had done. Proudly you returned to your brother's house, and left me alone . . . for weeks . . . not knowing now, in whom to believe since you refused to confide in me." Sir Percy's voice shook as he spoke and it touched her deeply.

"Aye, the madness of my pride," she said sadly. "Hardly had I left than I was sorry. But when I returned, I found you so changed as if you did not love me any more."

He did not respond to this, but now she knew his very coldness was a mask, a pretence. The trouble, the sorrow she had gone through last night, suddenly came back to her mind, but no longer with bitterness, rather with a feeling that this man, who loved her would help to bear the burden.

"Sir Percy," she said and her voice was shaking, "I am in trouble and I need your help."

"I pray you, Madame," he said, while his voice shook almost as much as hers, "in what way can I serve you?"

"Percy – Armand is in deadly danger. A letter of his written to Sir Andrew Ffoulkes has fallen into the hands of a spy. He could be arrested as a traitor and sent to the guillotine. It is horrible. I do not know what to do."

Then the tears came and she tottered, ready to fall, and leaning against the stone balustrade, she buried her face in her hands and sobbed bitterly.

"Begad, Madame," said Sir Percy gently, as Marguerite continued to sob hysterically, "will you dry your tears? I cannot bear to see you cry. What can I do?"

"Can you do anything for Armand?" she said, sweetly and simply. "You have so much influence at court, so many friends."

"Should you not seek first the influence of your French friend, Monsieur Chauvelin? He is, after all, the representative of the Republican Government of France."

"I cannot ask him, Percy. I wish I dared to tell you but, but . . . he has put a price on Armand's head."

She had not the courage to tell him the whole story — how she had suffered and how her hand had been forced. He might not understand; his love might never come back.

He wished she would give him the confidence which her foolish pride held back. He longed to kiss away her tears, but he had been hurt by her before. He had his pride as well and so he just said quietly, "Since it distresses you, we will not speak of it. As to Armand, have no fear. I pledge you my word that he shall be safe. And now, Madame, the hour is late, and you must be tired. Your women will be waiting for you upstairs."

He stood aside to allow her to pass, and, as he bowed low, she went sadly up the terrace steps.

Hot tears again surged to her eyes and, as she did not want him to see them, she went quickly inside, and ran as fast as she could up to her own rooms.

If she had only turned back then, she would have seen something which would have made her own sufferings seem light and easy to bear — a strong, proud man, blindly, passionately in love, and as soon as her light footsteps had died away within the house, he knelt down upon the terrace steps, and in the very madness of his love he kissed one by one the places where her small foot had trodden, and the stone balustrade there, where her tiny hand had rested last.

CHAPTER 17

Farewell

When Marguerite reached her room, she found her maid terribly anxious about her.

"Your ladyship will be so tired," said the poor woman, whose own eyes were half closed with sleep. "It is past five o'clock."

"*You* must be tired, Louise," said Marguerite, kindly. "Go to bed now, I will manage very well."

Louise was only too glad to obey. She took off her mistress's gorgeous ball dress, and wrapped her up in a soft billowy gown.

"Does your ladyship wish for anything else?" she asked when that was done.

"No, nothing more. Put out the lights as you go out."

"Yes, my lady. Good night, my lady."

"Good night, Louise."

When the maid was gone, Marguerite drew aside the curtains and threw open the windows. The garden and the river beyond were flooded with rosy light. Far away to the east, the rays of the rising sun had changed the rose into vivid gold. The lawn was deserted now, and Marguerite looked down upon the terrace where she had stood a few minutes ago trying to win back a man's love.

Her husband had not responded, but she loved him still. And now that she looked back upon the last few months of misunderstandings and loneliness, she realized that she had never ceased to love him; that deep down in her heart she had always vaguely felt that his silly laugh and lazy ways were nothing but a mask; that the real man, the man she had fallen in love with, was there still and that behind his

80

apparently slow wits there was a certain something, which he kept hidden from all the world, and most especially from her.

Absorbed in her thoughts, she sank into a chair and dozed off into a troubled sleep. She was aroused by the sound of footsteps and subdued voices and looking towards the door, she saw something white which had been pushed under it. It was a letter. She stooped to pick it up and saw that the letter was addressed to herself in her husband's large, businesslike-looking handwriting. What could he have to say to her now which could not be said in the morning?

She tore off the envelope and read –

> I am forced to leave for the North immediately, so I beg your pardon that I cannot bid you goodbye. My business may keep me a week. I kiss your hand.
> I am your humble servant.
> > Percy Blakeney.

She ran to the window and was just in time to see her husband, accompanied by a groom, galloping out of the gates.

She knew he had not been called to the North. There had been no letters, no couriers before they left for the opera. So it must be something to do with Armand. He had promised. Her brain was in a turmoil; she lay down on the bed and, exhausted, fell asleep.

CHAPTER 18

The Mysterious Device

The day was well advanced when Marguerite woke, refreshed by her long sleep. Louise had brought her some fresh milk and a dish of fruit, and she partook of this simple breakfast with a hearty appetite.

Thoughts crowded thick and fast in her mind as she munched her grapes; most of them went galloping away after the tall, erect figure of her husband, whom she had watched riding out of sight more than five hours ago.

Louise came in to tell her that the groom had come back with Sir Percy's horse Sultan and had said that he thought his master was going to board the *Day Dream* which was lying just below London Bridge.

Marguerite was puzzled and somewhat anxious. Louise helped her dress and she prepared to go downstairs. She crossed the landing outside her own suite of apartments, and stood still for a moment at the head of the fine oak staircase, which led to the lower floor. On her left were her husband's apartments, a suite of rooms which she practically never entered.

They consisted of bedroom, dressing and reception room, and, at the extreme end of the landing, a small study, which, when Sir Percy was not using it, was always kept locked. His own special and confidential valet, Frank, had charge of this room. No one was ever allowed to go inside. My lady had never cared to do so, and the other servants had, of course, not dared to break this hard-and-fast rule.

Marguerite glanced along he corridor. Frank was evidently busy with his master's rooms, for most of the doors stood open, the door of the study among the others.

A sudden, burning, childish curiosity seized her to have a peep at Sir Percy's sanctum. She, of course, was not forbidden to go in if she ever wished to do so, and Frank, would, of course, not dare to oppose her. Still, she hoped that the valet would be busy in one of the other rooms, so that she might have that one quick peep in secret without being disturbed.

Gently, on tiptoe, she crossed the landing and, like Bluebeard's wife, trembling half with excitement and wonder, she paused a moment summoning up the courage to go in.

The door was ajar and she could not see anything within. She pushed the door a little: there was no sound: Frank was evidently not there, and she walked boldly in.

At once she was struck by the severe simplicity of everything around her: the heavy, dark curtains, the massive oak furniture, the one or two maps on the wall, in no way reminded her of the lazy man-about-town, the lover of racecourses, the dandified leader of fashion whom most people believed to be Sir Percy Blakeney.

There was no sign here, at any rate, of hurried departure. Everything was in its place, not a scrap of paper littered the floor, not a cupboard or drawer was left open. The curtains were drawn aside, and through the open window the fresh morning air was streaming in.

Facing the window, and well into the centre of the room, stood a heavy businesslike desk, which looked as if it had seen much service. On the wall to the left of the desk, reaching almost from floor to ceiling, was a large full-length portrait of a handsome woman – Percy's mother – fair like her son.

Marguerite studied the portrait, for it interested her and she could see a strong likeness between mother and son. After that, she turned again and looked at the desk. It was covered with a mass of papers, all neatly tied and labelled which looked like accounts and receipts in perfect order. It had never before occurred to Marguerite to wonder how Sir Percy, who was thought to have no brains, looked after the vast fortune which his father had left him. But it also strengthened her belief that he had, for some reason, all this time been deliberately playing a part. What could this reason be? Marguerite was horribly puzzled and a nameless fear came upon her. She felt cold and uncomfortable suddenly in this severe and dark room. Apart from the portrait of Percy's mother, there were no pictures on the walls, only a couple of maps, both of parts of France, one of the North coast and the other of the region round Paris. What did her husband want with those?

Her head began to ache, she turned away from this strange room which she had entered, and which she did not understand. She did not wish Frank to find her there, and with a last look round, she once more turned to the door. As she did so, her foot knocked against a small object, which had apparently been lying close to the desk, on the carpet, and which now went rolling right across the room.

She stooped to pick it up. It was a solid gold ring, with a flat shield, on which was engraved a small device.

Marguerite turned it over in her fingers, and then studied the engraving on the shield. It represented a small star-shaped flower. She knew what it was. She had seen it on a small piece of paper at Lord Grenville's ball.

CHAPTER 19

The Scarlet Pimpernel

With the ring tightly clutched in her hand, Marguerite ran out of the room, down the stairs, and out into the garden, where, alone with the flowers, and the river and the birds, she could look again at the ring and study the star-shaped flower more closely.

She sat down beneath the shade of an overhanging syca-more tree. Her thoughts were in a whirl. Many people wore the scarlet pimpernel device out of admiration for the man himself. She herself had worn it. Why should her husband not have chosen the device as a seal-ring? Besides, what connection could there be between her dandified husband, with his fine clothes and lazy ways and the daring plotter who rescued French victims from beneath the very eyes of the leaders of a bloodthirsty revolution?

But then again, why had he departed so suddenly? She knew from the Comtesse that the Scarlet Pimpernel had pledged his honour to bring the fugitive Comte de Tournay out of France. She knew, too, that Sir Percy had promised that her brother Armand would be safe. Could not both these ventures be the cause of his journey?

If this was so, and Sir Percy was the Scarlet Pimpernel, she had betrayed her husband! She thought that Chauvelin had failed to discover the identity of his opponent, but she could not be sure. Perhaps by tomorrow Sir Percy would be in France and perhaps he had gone to his death.

As she sat there in her agony, a groom came running round the house towards his mistress. He carried a sealed letter in his hand.

"What is that?" asked Marguerite.

"A letter, just come by runner, my lady."

Marguerite took the letter and turned it over in her trembling fingers.

"Who sent it?" she said.

"The runner said, my lady," replied the groom "that his orders were to deliver this, and that your ladyship would understand from whom it came."

Marguerite tore open the envelope. She knew what it was.

It was the letter written by Armand St Just to Sir Andrew Ffoulkes – the letter which Chauvelin's spies had stolen at The Fisherman's Rest and which Chauvelin had held as a rod over her to enforce her obedience.

Now he had kept his word – he had sent her back the letter which could have sent her brother to his death. This could only mean that he was on the track of the Scarlet Pimpernel.

Marguerite felt sick and faint, but she summoned up all her courage. There was yet much to be done.

"Bring that runner here to me," she said to the servant, calmly. "He has not gone?"

"No, my lady."

The groom departed and soon returned, followed by the runner who had brought the letter.

"Who gave you this packet?" asked Marguerite.

"A gentleman, my lady," replied the man, "at The Rose and Thistle inn opposite Charing Cross. He said you would understand."

"At The Rose and Thistle? What was he doing?"

"He was waiting for the coach, your ladyship, which he had ordered."

"The coach?"

"Yes, my lady. A special coach he had ordered. I understood from his man that he was going straight to Dover."

"Thank you. You may go." Then she turned to the groom: "My coach and the four swiftest horses in the stables, to be ready at once."

The groom and runner went off quickly. Marguerite remained for a moment standing on the lawn quite alone. Her hands were clasped and her lips moved as she murmured pathetically –

"What's to be done? What's to be done? How can I find him? Oh God, grant me light!"

But this was no time for remorse and despair. By her own blindness she had sinned; now she must repay, not by sorrowing over the past, but by prompt and useful action.

Percy had started for Calais, utterly unconscious of the fact that his most deadly enemy was on his heels. He had set sail early that morning from London Bridge. Provided he had a favourable wind, he would probably be in France within twenty-four hours; no doubt he had reckoned on the wind when he chose this route.

Chauvelin, on the other hand, would post to Dover, charter a vessel there, and probably reach Calais much about the same time.

Once in Calais, Percy would meet all those who were eagerly waiting for the noble and brave Scarlet Pimpernel, who had come to rescue them from a horrible and undeserved death. With Chauvelin following his every movement, Percy would thus not only be putting his own life in danger, but the lives of the old Comte de Tournay and the other fugitives who were waiting for him and trusting in him. There was also Armand who had gone to meet de Tournay secure in the knowledge that the Scarlet Pimpernel was watching over his safety.

All these lives, and the life of her husband, lay in Marguerite's hands, and these she must do all in her power to save.

Unfortunately, she would not know where to find her husband, while Chauvelin, in stealing the papers at Dover from Sir Andrew and Lord Tony, had the whole rescue plan in his hands. Above everything she *must* warn Percy. He would never abandon those who trusted in him, but he might be able to make a new plan. If he failed, they would die together.

Strong in her resolution, she made her plans. She would go and find Sir Andrew Ffoulkes first; he was Percy's best friend, and Marguerite remembered with a thrill the devotion with which the young man always spoke of his mysterious leader. If anyone could help, he would. Her coach was ready. A change of clothes and she could be on her way.

Without haste, but without hesitation, she walked quietly into the house.

CHAPTER 20

The Friend

Less than half an hour later, Marguerite sat inside her coach which was bearing her swiftly to London. A courier had been sent on ahead to order a fresh relay of horses at Faversham.

She had changed into a dark travelling costume and provided herself with money – Sir Percy always made sure she had plenty at her disposal – and had started on her way. She did not delude herself with false hopes: Chauvelin would never have sent her back Armand's letter unless he was sure in his own mind that he knew the identity of the Scarlet Pimpernel. Sir Percy Blakeney was the man whose death he had sworn to bring about. She, Marguerite, would give her heart's blood now to defend her husband and would willingly give her life for his.

She had ordered her coach to drive her to The Crown inn; once there, she told her coachman to give the horses food and rest. Then she ordered a chair, and had herself carried to the house in Pall Mall where Sir Andrew Ffoulkes lived.

Among all Percy's friends who were enrolled under his daring banner, she felt that she would prefer to confide in Sir Andrew Ffoulkes. He had always been her friend, and now his love for her former school friend, little Suzanne, had brought him closer to her still. She hoped he would be at home.

She was lucky. His servant showed her immediately upstairs to Sir Andrew's comfortable bachelor's chambers, and she was ushered into a small, though luxuriously furnished dining room. A moment or two later Sir Andrew himself appeared.

He had evidently been much startled when he heard who his lady visitor was, for he looked anxiously – even suspiciously – at Marguerite as he bowed before her.

Marguerite returned his bow with a curtsey; they both sat down and she began very calmly –

"Sir Andrew, there is no time to lose. You must take certain things I am going to tell you for granted. These things are not important, but what *is* important is that your leader and comrade, the Scarlet Pimpernel, my husband Sir Percy Blakeney, is in deadly peril."

Sir Andrew, completely taken by surprise went very pale. She continued – "No matter how I know this. Thank God I do, and that perhaps it is not too late to save him. Unfortunately, I cannot do this quite alone, and therefore have come to you for help."

"Lady Blakeney," said the young man, trying to recover himself, "I . . ."

"Let me explain," she interrupted. "This is how the matter stands: When Chauvelin, the agent of the French Government, and his spies stole your papers that night in Dover when you and Lord Tony were assaulted and taken prisoner, he found among them the plans for the rescue of the Comte de Tournay and others among them. The Scarlet Pimpernel – Percy, my husband, has gone on this errand himself today.

"Chauvelin knows that the Scarlet Pimpernel and Percy Blakeney are one and the same person. He will follow him to Calais, and there will lay hands on him. Even King George will not be able to save him then and those he has gone to rescue, who trusted him, will share the same fate."

Sir Andrew looked appalled, but he remained silent.

"You do not trust me," she said passionately. "Oh God! Cannot you see that I am in deadly earnest?" She seized the young man by the shoulders, forcing him to look straight at her. "Do I look like a woman who would betray her own husband?"

"There is something I have to know," said the young man, looking searchingly into her blue eyes. "Whose hand helped to guide Monsieur Chauvelin to the knowledge which you say he possesses?"

"Mine," she said quickly. "I admit it; I will not lie to you, for I wish you to trust me absolutely. But I had no idea – how *could* I have – of the identity of the Scarlet Pimpernel, and my brother's safety was to be my prize if I succeeded in helping Chauvelin track down the Scarlet Pimpernel."

Sir Andrew felt his position to be a very awkward one. The oath he had taken before his leader and comrade was one of obedience and secrecy, and yet the beautiful woman, who was asking him to trust her, was undoubtedly in earnest; his friend and leader was equally undoubtedly in fearful danger.

"Lady Blakeney," he said at last, "I do not know where my duty lies. Tell me what you wish me to do. There are nineteen of us ready to lay down our lives for the Scarlet Pimpernel if he is in danger."

"Come with me to Calais! I must get to him. I cannot go alone."

"You cannot go alone and I am needed there too," said Sir Andrew. "I await your orders."

"I knew I was right to come to you. Listen: My coach is ready to take me to Dover. Follow me as swiftly as horses

90

can take you. We will meet at nightfall at The Fisherman's Rest. Chauvelin would avoid it, as he is known there, and I think it would be safest. We will charter a schooner at Dover, and cross over during the night. If you would be willing, you could disguise yourself as my servant. That way you should escape detection."

"I am entirely at your service, Madame," replied the young man earnestly. "I trust to God that we will sight the *Day Dream* before we reach Calais. With Chauvelin at his heels, every step the Scarlet Pimpernel takes on French soil is dangerous."

"God grant it, Sir Andrew. Farewell now and thank you. We meet tonight at Dover! It will be a race between Chauvelin and me across the Channel tonight and the prize will be the life of the Scarlet Pimpernel!"

He kissed her hand and escorted her to her chair. A quarter of an hour later she was back at The Crown inn, where her coach and horses were ready and waiting for her. The next moment they thundered along the London streets and straight on to the Dover road at maddening speed.

The perilous adventure had begun.

CHAPTER 21

Suspense

It was late into the night when she at last reached The Fisherman's Rest. She had done the whole journey in less than eight hours, thanks to the numerous changes of horses and the skill of the coachman.

The arrival of Lady Blakeney in the middle of the night caused a considerable flutter at The Fisherman's Rest. Sally jumped hastily out of bed, and Mr Jellyband was at great pains to make his important guest comfortable. If they were surprised that Lady Blakeney should arrive alone in the middle of the night, they did not show it, but busied themselves looking after her.

"Will your ladyship stay the night?" asked pretty Miss Sally, who had already started to lay a snow-white cloth on the table, before she prepared a simple supper for her ladyship.

"No, not the whole night," replied Marguerite. "At any rate, I shall not want any room but this, if I can have it to myself for an hour or two."

"It is at your ladyship's service," said honest Jellyband, not allowing himself to show any astonishment at my lady's request.

"I shall be crossing over at the first turn of the tide," said Marguerite, "and in the first schooner I can get. But my coachman and men will stay the night and probably several days longer, so I hope you will make them comfortable."

"Yes, my lady; I'll look after them. Shall Sally bring your ladyship some supper?"

"Yes, please. Put something cold on the table, and as soon as Sir Andrew Ffoulkes comes, show him in here."

"Yes, my lady."

Honest Jellyband's face now expressed distress in spite of himself. He had great regard for Sir Percy Blakeney and did not like to see his lady running away with young Sir Andrew. Of course it was no business of his and Mr Jellyband was no gossip, so he put it down to her ladyship being one of them "furriners".

"Don't sit up, honest Jellyband," continued Marguerite briefly, "nor you either, Mistress Sally. Sir Andrew may be late."

Mr Jellyband was only too willing that Sally should go to bed. He was beginning not to like these goings-on at all. Still, Lady Blakeney would pay handsomely for the accommodation, and it certainly was no business of his.

Sally arranged a simple supper of cold meat, wine and fruit on the table, then with a respectful curtsey, she retired, wondering in her little mind why her ladyship looked so serious, when she was about to elope with a handsome young man.

Marguerite knew she was in for a long wait. Sir Andrew, who would have to provide himself with a servant's clothes, could not possibly reach Dover for at least a couple of hours, however hard he rode.

The beautiful warm October day had turned into a rough and cold night and she was glad of the cheerful blaze in the hearth. Gradually as time wore on the weather became more rough, and the sound of the great breakers against the Admiralty Pier, though some distance from the inn, came to her as the noise of muffled thunder.

The wind was becoming boisterous, rattling the leaded windows and the massive doors of the old house. It shook the trees outside and roared down the vast chimney. Marguerite wondered if the wind would be favourable for her journey. She had no fear of the storm, and would have braved worse risks rather than delay the crossing by even an hour.

A sudden commotion outside roused her from her thoughts. Sir Andrew Ffoulkes had evidently arrived in mad haste, for she could hear his horse's hoofs thundering on the flagstones outside, then Mr Jellyband's sleepy, yet cheerful, tones bidding him welcome.

For a moment Marguerite realized the awkwardness of her situation and wondered what Mr Jellyband must think about this meeting. She could see the funny side, though and a little smile began playing round the corners of her mouth, and when, presently, Sir Andrew, in the clothes of a servant entered the coffee room, she was able to greet him with a merry laugh.

"Faith! Monsieur, my attendant," she said, "I am satisfied with your appearance!"

Mr Jellyband had followed Sir Andrew, looking strangely

perplexed. To see Sir Andrew in disguise confirmed his worst suspicions. Without a smile upon his jovial face, he drew the cork from the bottle of wine, set the chairs ready, and prepared to wait on them.

"Thanks, honest friend," said Marguerite, who was still smiling at the thought of what the worthy fellow must be thinking at that very moment, "we shall require nothing more, and this is for all the trouble you have been put to on our account."

She handed two or three gold pieces to Jellyband, who took them respectfully and prepared to retire.

"Stay, Lady Blakeney," said Sir Andrew as Jellyband was about to leave the room. "I am afraid we shall have to remain here for a time. I am sorry to say we cannot cross over tonight."

"Not cross over tonight?" she repeated in amazement. "But we must. We must go tonight."

"I am afraid it is impossible. There is a nasty storm blowing from France, the wind is dead against us. We cannot possibly sail until it has changed."

Marguerite became deadly pale. She had not foreseen this. Nature herself was playing her a horrible, cruel trick. Percy was in danger, and she could not go to him, because the wind happened to blow from the coast of France.

"But we must go! – we must," she repeated! "Can't you find a way, Sir Andrew?"

"I have been down to the shore already," said the young man, "and had a talk to one or two skippers. It is quite impossible to set sail tonight, so every sailor assured me. No one," he added, looking meaningly at Marguerite, "*no one* could possibly put out of Dover tonight."

Marguerite at once understood what he meant. *No one* included Chauvelin as well as herself. She nodded pleasantly to Jellyband.

"Well then, I must be patient," she said to him. "Have you rooms free?"

"Oh yes, your ladyship. I have two rooms both quite ready."

"Well done then, honest Jelly," said Sir Andrew, clapping his worthy host on the back. "You unlock both those rooms, and leave our candles here on the dresser. I vow you are dead with sleep and her ladyship must have some supper before she retires. Have no fear, friend. There is nothing wrong and Sir Percy will reward you well if you see to her ladyship's privacy and comfort."

Mr Jellyband's countenance brightened at the mention of Sir Percy's name.

"I'll go and see to it at once, sir," he said and went off looking a good deal happier.

"Now tell me," said Marguerite eagerly, as soon as Mr Jellyband had gone from the room, "tell me all your news."

"There is nothing much else to tell you, Lady Blakeney," replied the young man. "The storm makes it quite impossible for any vessel to put out of Dover this tide. But this could be a blessing in disguise. If *we* cannot cross, neither can Chauvelin."

"He may have left before the storm broke out."

"As to that, the sailors I spoke to all assured me that no schooner had put out of Dover for several hours: on the other hand I found out that a stranger had arrived by coach this afternoon, and had, like myself, made some inquiries about crossing over to France."

"Then Chauvelin is still in Dover?"

"Undoubtedly. Now come and sit at the table and have some supper."

As they ate and drank, Sir Andrew made her almost happy by talking to her about her husband. He told her about some of the daring escapes the brave Scarlet Pimpernel had arranged for the poor French fugitives who were being driven out of the country by a bloody revolution. Her eyes glowed as he told her how her husband had saved them from the murderous, ever-ready guillotine.

He even made her smile by telling her of the Scarlet Pimpernel's quaint and many disguises which had got him through the barricades of Paris. This last time the escape of the Comtesse de Tournay and her children had been a veritable masterpiece – and Blakeney, disguised as a hideous old market-woman, in filthy cap and straggling grey locks, was a sight to make the gods laugh.

Marguerite laughed heartily as Sir Andrew tried to describe Percy's appearance and the problem of being so tall which made disguising himself doubly difficult.

It was long past midnight when Marguerite retired to rest. She could not sleep and the sound of the distant breakers made her heart ache with melancholy. Her thoughts were all of her husband and how she could save him.

CHAPTER 22

Calais

When Marguerite came downstairs in the morning, she found Sir Andrew Ffoulkes sitting in the coffee room. He had been out half an hour earlier and had gone to the Admiralty Pier to find that no vessels could put out of Dover yet. The storm was then at its fullest, and the tide was on the turn. If the wind did not lessen or change, they would have to wait another ten or twelve hours until the next tide before a start could be made. And the storm had not lessened, the wind had not changed, and the tide was rapidly going out. When the storm finally died down, it was too far out to allow a vessel to put to sea. Though he tried to conceal it, Sir Andrew was as anxious as Marguerite and they spent many wearisome hours waiting.

There was one happy interval in this long, anxious day, and that was when Sir Andrew went down once again to the pier, and presently came back to tell Marguerite that he had chartered a quick schooner, whose skipper was ready to put to sea the moment the tide was favourable.

From that moment, Marguerite began to cast off her gloom and at last at five o'clock in the afternoon she went down to the pier followed by Sir Andrew in the guise of her servant carrying her cases.

Once on board, the keen, fresh sea air revived her; the breeze was just strong enough to swell nicely the sails of the *Foam Crest* as she cut her way merrily towards the open sea.

The sunset was glorious after the storm, and Marguerite, as she watched the white cliffs of Dover gradually disappearing from view, felt more at peace, and once more almost hopeful.

Sir Andrew was full of kind attentions, and she felt how lucky she had been to have him by her side in this, her great trouble.

Gradually the grey coast of France began to emerge from the fast-gathering evening mists. One or two lights could be seen flickering, and the spires of several churches seemed to rise out of the surrounding haze.

Half an hour later Marguerite had landed upon the French shore. She was back in that country where at this very moment men slaughtered their fellow creatures by the hundreds, and sent innocent women and children in thousands to the block.

The people themselves seemed to have changed. The men all wore red caps – in various stages of cleanliness – but all with the tricolour cockade pinned on the left-hand side. Marguerite noticed with a shudder that instead of the laughing, merry countenances habitual to her own countrymen, their faces now wore a look of sly distrust. Every man nowadays was a spy upon his fellows and even the women went about with a curious look of fear and hatred lurking in their eyes.

Sir Andrew led Marguerite right across town, to the

other side from where they had landed, and on the way towards Cap Gris-Nez. The streets were narrow, winding and mostly evil-smelling with a mixture of stale fish and damp cellar odours. There had been heavy rain during the storm last night, and sometimes Marguerite sank ankle deep in the mud, for the roads were not lighted except by the occasional glimmer from a lamp inside a house.

But she did not heed any of these small discomforts: "We may meet Blakeney at the Chat Gris," Sir Andrew had said, when they landed, and she was walking as if on a carpet of rose leaves, for she was going to meet him almost at once.

At last they reached their destination. Sir Andrew evidently knew the road for he had not asked his way from anyone. It was too dark then for Marguerite to notice the outside aspect of the house. The Chat Gris, as Sir Andrew had called it, was evidently a small wayside inn on the outskirts of Calais, and on the way to Cap Gris-Nez. It lay some distance from the coast, for the sound of the sea seemed to come from afar.

Sir Andrew knocked at the door with the knob of his cane, and from within they heard a sort of grunt and the muttering of a number of oaths. Sir Andrew knocked again, this time more loudly: more swearing was heard, and then shuffling steps seemed to draw near the door. Presently this was thrown open, and Marguerite found herself on the threshold of the most dilapidated, most squalid room she had ever seen in her life.

The paper, such as it was, was hanging from the walls in strips; there did not seem to be a single piece of furniture in the room which could be called whole. Most of the chairs had broken backs, others had no seats to them; one corner of the table was propped up with a bundle of firewood where the fourth leg had been broken.

In one corner of the room there was a huge hearth, over which hung a stockpot with a smell of hot soup coming from it. On one side of the room, high up in the wall, there was a kind of loft, before which hung a tattered blue-and-white checked curtain. A rickety set of steps led up to this loft.

On the great bare walls, with their colourless dirty paper, there were chalked up at intervals in great bold characters, the words: "*Liberté – Egalité – Fraternité.*"

The place was dimly lit by an evil-smelling oil lamp, which hung from the rickety rafters of the ceiling. It all looked so horribly squalid, so dirty and uninviting that Marguerite hardly dared to cross the threshold.

Sir Andrew, however, had stepped boldly forward.

"English travellers, citizen," he said, speaking in French.

An elderly, heavily built peasant had come to the door. He was dressed in a dirty blue blouse, heavy clogs, from which wisps of straw stuck out all round, shabby blue trousers, and the usual red cap with the tricolour cockade that proclaimed him a supporter of the revolutionary government. He carried a short wooden pipe, filled with foul tobacco, and looked with some suspicion and a great deal of contempt at the two travellers, muttered "Cursed English!" and spat upon the ground to show his independence. However, he stood aside to let them enter, no doubt well aware that the "cursed English" had well-filled purses.

"Oh, lud!" said Marguerite, as she advanced into the room, holding her handkerchief to her dainty nose. "What a dreadful hole! Are you sure this is the place?"

"This is the place, sure enough," replied the young man as, with his handkerchief, he dusted a chair for Marguerite to sit on; "but I vow I never saw a more villainous hole."

The landlord of the Chat Gris whose name was Brogard had taken no further notice of his guests. He concluded that presently they would order supper, but in the meanwhile it was not for a free French citizen to show respect or even politeness to anyone, however smartly they might be dressed.

By the hearth sat a huddled-up figure, dressed apparently in rags. It was an old woman and she was sitting mumbling to herself, and from time to time stirring the brew in her stockpot.

"Hey, my friend," said Sir Andrew at last, "we should like some supper. My mistress has not tasted food for several hours."

Brogard spat on the floor again, and then muttering, he went very slowly to a dresser which stood in a corner of the room. From this he took an old pewter soup tureen and slowly, and without a word, he handed it to his wife, who, in the same silence, began filling the tureen with the soup out of her stockpot.

Marguerite had watched all these preparations with absolute horror and Sir Andrew, seeing this, said, "I wish I could offer you a better meal, but I think you will find the soup eatable and the wine good; these people wallow in dirt but live well as a rule."

Brogard was slowly pursuing his gruesome preparations; he had placed a couple of spoons, and two glasses, on the table, both of which Sir Andrew took the precaution of wiping carefully.

Brogard had also produced a bottle of wine and some bread, and Marguerite made an effort to draw her chair to the table and to make some pretence at eating. Sir Andrew, still in his role of servant, stood behind her chair.

The soup certainly was not bad; it smelt and tasted good. Marguerite might have enjoyed it, but for the horrible surroundings. She insisted that Sir Andrew should sit down with her, broke the bread and drank some of the wine.

"They will only think it is an English custom," she said. "They are paying no attention to us."

Sir Andrew took Marguerite's advice and sat next to her at table. They both made noble efforts to deceive one another by pretending to eat and drink. Presently Sir Andrew tapped Brogard on the shoulder and said –

"Do you see many English travellers around these parts, my friend?"

Brogard looked round at him, over his shoulder, puffed away at his pipe for a moment or two as if he was in no hurry, then muttered, "Sometimes. Yes."

"Ah!" said Sir Andrew pleasantly, "English travellers always know where they can get good wine, eh! my friend? My mistress would like to know if by any chance you happen to have seen a great friend of hers, an English gentleman who often comes to Calais on business. He is tall and recently was on his way to Paris - my mistress hoped she might see him in Calais."

Brogard took his time, then he said very slowly –

"Tall Englishman? – Today! Yes."

"You have seen him?" asked Sir Andrew, carelessly.

"Yes, today," muttered Brogard, sullenly. Then he quietly took Sir Andrew's hat from a chair close by, put it on his own head, tugged at his dirty blouse, and generally tried to express in pantomime that the man he had seen wore very fine clothes. "Cursed aristo!" he muttered, "that tall Englishman!"

"Ah yes, that sounds like my lady's friend. He always wears fine clothes. And he has gone, you say?"

"He went ... yes ... but he is coming back ... here – he ordered supper . . ."

Sir Andrew put his hand with a quick gesture of warning upon Marguerite's arm; it came none too soon, for the next moment her joy would have betrayed her.

"Where is he now? Do you know?" she asked eagerly, placing her dainty white hand upon the dirty sleeve of his blue blouse.

"He went to get a horse and cart," said Brogard, as, with a surly gesture, he shook off from his arm that pretty hand which princes had been proud to kiss.

"At what time did he go?"

But Brogard had had enough. He was the equal of anybody and would show these rich English people.

"I don't know," he said rudely. "He came today. He

ordered supper. He went out. He will come back. *Voilà!*" And with that he shuffled out of the room, banging the door behind him.

CHAPTER 23

Hope

"We had better leave him alone," said Sir Andrew, "we shall not get anything more out of him and we might arouse his suspicions. One never knows what spies may be lurking around these Godforsaken places."

"What care I," she replied lightly, "now that I know my husband is safe and I shall see him soon! Pray God that Chauvelin and his gang have not yet arrived."

"That I fear we do not know, Madame."

"What do you mean?"

"He was at Dover the same time that we were."

"Held up by the same storm which kept us from starting."

"Exactly. I saw him on the beach not five minutes before we embarked. He was disguised as a priest and I heard him bargaining for a vessel to take him swiftly to Calais. He must have set sail soon after us."

Marguerite's face had quickly lost its look of joy. With Chauvelin on his track, the terrible danger in which Percy stood now that he was in France became clear to her. Chauvelin knew the rescue plan and it was too late to communicate with Armand or to send further instructions to the fugitives. They would meet at the mysterious hut and there Sir Percy would come to them and there the trap would be closed on him and on them.

But both Sir Andrew and Marguerite knew that Sir Percy would never give up the people he had promised to save, still he could at least be warned. They had a short time in which to do it.

Sir Andrew bribed Brogard to allow Marguerite a quiet room where she could wait while he went out to pick up such information as he could.

Brogard consented with a bad grace and pointed over his shoulder at the attic which was up some steps above the room where they were.

"Nothing could be better," said Marguerite in English. The attic would be a perfect place in which to watch without being seen.

"I dare not kiss your hand, Madame," said Sir Andrew, as she began to mount the steps, "since I am supposed to be your servant, but I pray you be of good cheer. If I do not come across Blakeney in half an hour, I shall return, expecting to find him here. We must be at least a half an hour ahead of Chauvelin."

"God grant that either you or I may have seen Percy by then," said Marguerite. "Good luck to you, friend! Have no fear for me."

Lightly she mounted the rickety wooden steps that led to the attic. Brogard paid no attention to her. She could make herself comfortable there or not, as she chose. Sir Andrew watched her until she reached the loft and sat down upon some straw. She pulled the tattered curtains across and the young man could see what a perfect observation post she was in.

He had paid Brogard well; the surly old innkeeper would have no object in betraying her. As he turned to go, he looked up again. Through the ragged curtains Marguerite's sweet face was peeping down at him. She was smiling.

CHAPTER 24

The Death-trap

The next quarter of an hour went by swiftly. In the room downstairs, Brogard had for a while busied himself with clearing the table, and rearranging it for another guest. Marguerite supposed the preparations were for Percy.

When the table was set, Brogard surveyed it with evident satisfaction. He dusted one of the chairs with the corner of his blouse, gave a stir to the stockpot, threw some wood on the fire, and slouched out of the room.

Marguerite had spread her travelling cloak over the straw and was reasonably comfortable. She was happy, knowing she would soon be with Percy, would be able to warn him, and tell him of her love.

Suddenly her ears caught the sound of distant footsteps drawing near; her heart gave a wild leap of joy. Was it Percy at last? No, the step did not seem quite as long, nor quite as firm as his: she also thought that she could hear two distinct sets of footsteps. Two strangers perhaps, coming in for a drink.

Marguerite did not have long to wonder. There was a loud call at the door, and the next moment it was violently thrown open from outside, while a rough, commanding voice shouted –

"Hey! Citizen Brogard; Holà."

She could not see the newcomers at first, but, through a hole in one of the curtains, she could observe part of the room below.

She heard Brogard's shuffling footsteps, as he came out of the inner room, muttering his usual string of oaths. On seeing the strangers, however, he paused in the middle of the room, well within sight of Marguerite, looked at them with even more withering contempt than he had bestowed upon his former guests, and spat on the floor.

Marguerite's heart seemed all at once to stop beating; her eyes were on one of the newcomers, who, at this point, had taken a quick step forward towards Brogard. He was dressed in the long coat, broad-brimmed hat, and buckled shoes usually worn by a French priest, but as he stood opposite the innkeeper, he threw open his coat for a moment, displaying the tricolour scarf of an official of the revolutionary government. Brogard cringed before him and his attitude changed completely. Humbly he awaited orders.

Marguerite could not see the face of the newcomer, which was shaded by his broad-brimmed hat, but she recognized the thin, bony hands, the slight stoop, the general look of the man. It was Chauvelin! Her blood seemed to freeze in her veins, and it was all she could do to stop herself fainting.

"A plate of soup and a bottle of wine," said Chauvelin abruptly to Brogard, "then clear out of here. I want to be alone."

Silently, and without any muttering this time, Brogard obeyed. Chauvelin sat down at the table which had been prepared for the tall Englishman, and the innkeeper served him in silence, dishing up the soup and pouring out the wine. The man who had entered with Chauvelin and whom Marguerite could not see, stood waiting close by the door.

At a sign from Chauvelin, Brogard had hurried back to the inner room and the man at the door was summoned.

Marguerite at once recognized him as Desgas, Chauvelin's secretary and confidential helper, whom she had often seen in Paris, in the days gone by.

This man crossed the room, and for a moment or two listened at the Brogards' door.

"Not listening?" asked Chauvelin.

"No, citizen."

"What about the English schooner?"

"She was lost sight of at sundown," replied Desgas, "but was then making west towards Cap Gris-Nez."

"Good. Now what did Captain Jutley say?"

"He assured me that all the orders you sent him last week have been obeyed. All the roads which meet at this place have been patrolled night and day ever since, and the beach and cliffs have been most rigorously searched and guarded."

"Does he know where this 'Père Blanchard's hut' is?"

"No, citizen, unfortunately. There are of course a number of fisherman's huts along this coast."

"Very well. Go back to Captain Jutley and ask him to send six extra men here and tell him the men are to keep the sharpest possible lookout for any stranger who may be walking, riding, or driving along the road or the beach, more especially for a tall stranger who cannot very well conceal his height except by stooping. He may be disguised. Is that clear?"

"Perfectly, citizen."

"Go now then. If the man we seek is seen, he is to be followed for he will perhaps lead us to the hut where the traitors are hiding. If he shows fight, there is to be no shooting. I want that tall stranger alive . . . if possible."

Chauvelin laughed as a devil might laugh. Marguerite could just see his face as he turned to speak to Desgas. There was so much hatred in it and in the pale, small eyes that the last hope died in her heart, for there would be no mercy.

Chauvelin pulled his chair closer to the table and Desgas went off. Marguerite could see the face of the enemy even better now that he had removed his hat and she wondered how so much hatred could lurk in one human being against another.

Suddenly, as she watched Chauvelin, a sound caught her ear which turned her very heart to stone. And yet there was nothing to horrify anyone, for it was merely the cheerful sound of someone singing lustily, "God save the King!"

CHAPTER 25

The Eagle and the Fox

Marguerite's breath stopped short; it was as if her life stood still for a moment while she listened to that voice and to that song. She knew who the singer was. Chauvelin, too, had heard the voice, for he darted a quick glance towards the door, then quickly took up his broad-brimmed hat and clapped it over his head.

"Long to reign over us
God save the King"

sang the voice more lustily then ever. The next moment the door was thrown open and there was dead silence for a second or so.

Marguerite could not see the door; she held her breath, trying to imagine what was happening.

Percy Blakeney on entering had, of course, at once caught sight of the *curé* at the table and he hesitated for less than five seconds. The next moment Marguerite saw his tall figure crossing the room, while he called in a loud, cheerful voice –

"Hello, there! No one about? Where's that fool Brogard?"

He wore the magnificent coat and riding suit which he had on when Marguerite saw him riding away at Richmond. He might have been on his way to visit the Prince of Wales, instead of deliberately running his head into a trap set for him by his deadliest enemy.

He stood for a moment in the middle of the room, then quietly walked to the table, and, jovially clapping the *curé* on the back, said in his own drawly, affected way –

"Odd's fish! It is Monsieur Chauvelin. I vow I never thought of meeting you here."

Chauvelin was putting a spoonful of soup into his mouth. He choked, his thin face became absolutely purple and he had a violent fit of coughing. There was no doubt that he was taken completely by surprise and was at a loss what to do.

Marguerite up in the loft had not moved. She had made a solemn promise to Sir Andrew not to speak to her husband before strangers and she would keep that promise, but to sit still and watch these two men together was a terrible trial of fortitude. She had heard Chauvelin give the orders for the patrolling of all the roads. She knew that if Percy now left the Chat Gris – in whatever direction he happened to go – he could not go far without being sighted by some of Captain Jutley's men on patrol. On the other hand, if he stayed, then Desgas would have time to come back with the half-dozen men Chauvelin had specially ordered. The trap was closing in and Marguerite could do nothing but watch and wonder.

Blakeney was solemnly patting Chauvelin on the back.

"I am so demmed sorry," he was saying cheerfully, "so very sorry. I seem to have upset you . . . eating soup, too . . . nasty, awkward thing, soup. A friend of mine died once . . . choked, just like you . . . with a spoonful of soup."

And he smiled shyly, good-humouredly, down at Chauvelin.

"Beastly hole this," he continued. "Hope you don't mind," he added apologetically, as he sat down on a chair close to the table and drew the soup tureen towards him. "That fool

Brogard seems to be asleep or something."

There was a second plate on the table; and he calmly helped himself to soup, then poured himself out a glass of wine.

Chauvelin kept his head. He stretched out his hand and said pleasantly –

"I am indeed charmed to see you, Sir Percy. You must excuse me. I thought you were on the other side of the Channel."

"And I was surprised to see *you* here. I would have known you anywhere in spite of the hat and wig and your costume."

Chauvelin changed the subject –

"And how is Lady Blakeney?"

Blakeney, with much deliberation, finished his plate of soup, drank his glass of wine and, for a moment, it seemed to Marguerite, glanced quickly round the room.

"Quite well, thank you," he said at last. Marguerite marvelled at his coolness as the two enemies continued to talk politely.

Presently Chauvelin, who was trying to conceal his impatience, took a quick look at his watch. Desgas would not be long; another two or three minutes, and this impudent Englishman would be secure in the keeping of half a dozen of Captain Jutley's most trusted men.

"You are in a hurry, sir," said Sir Percy, "I pray you, take no heed of me. My time's my own."

He rose from the table and dragged a chair to the hearth.

Marguerite was terribly tempted to go to him, for time was getting on; Desgas might be back at any moment with his men. Percy did not know that. How horrible it all was and how helpless she felt.

Chauvelin also pulled a chair to the hearth, in such a way that he had a good view of the door and he did not take his eyes off it. Marguerite's thoughts were centred there too, for her ears had suddenly caught through the stillness of the night, the sound of marching some distance away.

It was Desgas and his men. Another three minutes and

110

they would be here. Another three minutes and the awful thing would have happened. The brave eagle would have fallen in the ferret's trap. She looked down and saw that, while the eyes of Chauvelin were on the door, Percy had risen and gone over to the table where plates, glasses, spoons, salt and pepper pots were scattered around. His back was turned to Chauvelin and from his pocket he had taken his snuffbox. Quickly and suddenly, he emptied the contents of the pepper pot into it.

Then Sir Percy turned with his silly laugh to Monsieur Chauvelin –

"Did you speak, sir?"

Chauvelin had been too intent on listening to the sound of those approaching footsteps to notice what his adversary was doing. He now pulled himself together, trying to appear casual and at his ease. "No, that is – what were you saying, Sir Percy?"

"I was saying," said Blakeney, going up to Chauvelin by the fire, "that my shop in Piccadilly has sold me better snuff this time than I have ever tasted. Will you honour me, Monsieur?"

He stood close to Chauvelin, holding out his snuffbox.

Chauvelin, who, as he told Marguerite once, had seen a trick or two in his day, had never dreamed of this one. With one ear fixed on those fast-approaching footsteps, one eye turned to that door where Desgas and his men would soon appear, he never even remotely guessed the trick which was being played on him.

He took a pinch of snuff.

Chauvelin felt as if his head would burst – sneeze after sneeze seemed nearly to choke him; he was blind, deaf, and dumb for the moment, and during that moment Blakeney quietly, without the slightest haste, took up his hat, took some money out of his pocket, which he left on the table, then calmly stalked out of the room. For the moment, the eagle had beaten the fox!

111

CHAPTER 26

The Old Man

Marguerite was trying to collect her scattered senses when she heard the grounding of arms outside, close to the door, and the voice of Desgas shouting "Halt!" to his men.

Chauvelin had partly recovered: his sneezing had become less violent, and he had struggled to his feet. He managed to reach the door just as Desgas knocked on the outside.

Chauvelin threw open the door, and before his secretary could say a word, he had managed to stammer, between two sneezes –

"The tall stranger – quick! – did any of you see him?"

"Where, citizen?" asked Desgas, in surprise.

"Here, man! Through that door! Not five minutes ago."

"We saw nothing, citizen! The moon is not yet up."

"And you are just five minutes too late, my friend," said Chauvelin, in a fury.

"But citizen . . ."

"You did what I ordered you to do," said Chauvelin impatiently. "I know that, but you were a precious long time about it. Fortunately, there's not much harm done, or it would have gone badly for you, Citizen Desgas."

Desgas turned a little pale. "What about the tall stranger?" he stammered.

"He was here, in this room, five minutes ago, having supper at that table. Damn his impudence! For obvious reasons, I could not tackle him alone and Brogard is too big a fool to be of any use; and so he got away. He has the strength of a bullock."

"He cannot go far without being sighted, citizen."

112

"You think so?"

"Captain Jutley sent forty men more for the patrol duty: twenty of them went down to the beach. He again assured me that the watch has been constant all day, and that no stranger could possibly get to the beach, or reach a boat, without being sighed."

"That's good. Do the men know their work?"

"They have had very clear orders, citizen: and I myself spoke to those who were about to start. They are to shadow – as secretly as possible – any stranger they may see, especially a tall stranger or someone who is stooping as if he wished to disguise his height."

"And if they *do* see him," said Chauvelin eagerly, "they must let him get to the Père Blanchard's hut, surround it and capture him."

"The men understand that, citizen, and also that, as soon as a tall stranger has been sighted, he must be shadowed, while one man is to turn straight back and report to you."

"That is right," said Chauvelin, rubbing his hands, well pleased.

"I have other news for you, citizen: a tall Englishman had a long conversation about three-quarters of an hour ago with an old man called Reuben about a horse and cart which he wished to hire and which had to be ready for him by eleven o'clock."

"It is past that now. Where does this old man Reuben live?"

"A few minutes' walk from this door."

"Send one of the men to find out if the stranger has driven off in Reuben's cart."

"Yes, citizen."

Desgas went off to give the necessary orders to one of his men and returned about five minutes later with a rather dirty looking old man. He was bent, and shuffled along with difficulty.

"This citizen tells me," said Chauvelin abruptly, "that

113

you know something of my friend, the tall Englishman, whom I desire to meet. You are Reuben?"

"No, citizen, I was with Reuben when a tall Englishman spoke to us on the road near here. He wanted to know if he could hire a horse and cart to go down along the St Martin road, to a place he wanted to reach tonight. We both offered our horses and carts, but he chose Reuben's."

"Have they started?"

"Yes, they started about five minutes ago."

"You have a horse and cart as well, then?" said Chauvelin.

"Yes, citizen, a better one – you are welcome to it."

"Could you take me to a place called the Père Blanchard's hut?"

"Yes, citizen," replied the old man, looking somewhat surprised at Chauvelin's knowledge.

"How far is the nearest village from here?"

"On the road which the Englishman took, Miquelon is the nearest village, not two leagues from here."

"If he wanted to go further, could he hire something else?"

"He could – if he ever got so far."

"Can you?"

"Try me," said the old man.

"I intend to do that," said Chauvelin, "but remember, if you are lying to me, two of my soldiers will give you a beating which you will not forget. On the other hand, if we find the Englishman either on the road or at the hut, you will be well rewarded."

The old man went off and Chauvelin called for his coat and boots. Then he changed from his priest's clothes and told Desgas to go back to Captain Jutley for yet more men. They were to come back as fast as they could and follow the cart with himself and the old man in it along the St Martin Road. He warned Desgas that there could be a hard fight and he must choose his men well. He must choose men who would take *his* revenge upon his enemy, the Scarlet Pimpernel.

CHAPTER 27

On the Track

Never for a moment did Marguerite Blakeney hesitate. The last sounds outside the Chat Gris had died away in the night, and the inn was quiet.

She waited a moment or two longer, then she quietly slipped down the broken stairs, wrapped her dark cloak closely round her and slipped out into the night.

It was fairly dark, but she could hear the horse and cart ahead of her and she hoped by keeping well within the shadow of the ditches which lined the road that she would not be seen by Desgas' men when they approached, or by the patrols which would be still on duty.

It was a long way to walk, but anxious and tired as she was, she thought she could keep up with the horse and cart especially when the horse had to be rested at the top of hills.

The road lay some distance from the sea, bordered on either side by shrubs and stunted trees, all turning away from the north, with their branches looking in the semi-darkness like stiff, ghostly hair, blown by a perpetual wind.

Fortunately the moon showed no desire to peep between the clouds, and Marguerite, hugging the edge of the road, and keeping close to the low line of shrubs, was fairly safe from view. Everything around her was so still: only from far, very far away, there came, like a long soft moan, the sound of the distant sea.

The air was cool and briny after the evil-smelling inn and the loneliness was absolute. Already the few dim lights of Calais lay far behind and there were no houses. Far away on

115

the right was the edge of the cliff, below it the rough beach, against which the incoming tide was dashing itself with its constant, distant murmur. Ahead of her was the rumble of wheels, bearing her husband's enemy to his triumph. Marguerite walked on the grass at the side of the road for safety. Her feet slipped and she kept up her pace as best she could.

Chauvelin, in the cart, was nursing comfortable thoughts. Soon the man who had for so long outwitted him would be in his power. Progress was slow, for the old horse could do little more than walk and Chauvelin was continually asking how far they were from Miquelon. To which his driver always replied, "Not very far, citizen."

Suddenly through the stillness, there could be heard the sound of horses' hoofs on the muddy road.

"They are soldiers," said the old man in an awed whisper.

"Stop a moment, I want to hear," said Chauvelin.

Marguerite had also heard the sound of galloping hoofs, coming towards the cart and towards herself. For some time she had been on the alert, thinking that Desgas and his squad would soon overtake them, but these came from the opposite direction, presumably from Miquelon. The darkness gave her sufficient cover. She saw that the cart had stopped, and very quietly she crept a little nearer.

Two men on horseback had halted beside the vehicle and she heard Chauvelin call out, "What news?"

She could hear their voices and the snorting of the horses quite well and, at the same time from behind her, some little distance off, the regular and measured tread of a body of advancing men: Desgas and his soldiers.

Chauvelin, having made sure who the horsemen were, was questioning them –

"Have you seen a tall stranger?"

"No, citizen, we have seen no tall stranger; we came by the edge of the cliff."

"Then?"

"Just beyond Miquelon we came across a fisherman's

116

hut. We thought at first it was empty, but then we saw some smoke coming out of a hole in the side. I dismounted and crept close to it. It was then empty, but in one corner of the hut there was a charcoal fire, and a couple of stools were also in the hut. I consulted with my comrades, and we decided that they should take cover with the horses, well out of sight, and that I should remain on the watch, which I did."

"Did you see anything?"

"About half an hour later, I heard voices, and presently two men came along towards the edge of the cliff; one was young, the other quite old. They were talking in a whisper to one another, and I could not hear what they said."

One was young, the other quite old. Marguerite's aching heart almost stopped as she listened. The two men could be her brother, Armand and the old Comte de Tournay.

"The two men went into the hut," continued the soldier, "and I crept nearer to it then. The hut is very roughly built, and I caught snatches of their conversation."

"Yes – quick. What did you hear?"

"The old man asked the young one if he were sure that was the right place. I could hear the young man saying he was certain that it was, and, by their conversation, I thought it sounded as if they were looking at some map or plan. I must have made a slight noise then, for the young man came to the door of the hut, and peered anxiously all round him. When he again joined his companion, they whispered so low that I could no longer hear them."

"And then what?" asked Chauvelin impatiently.

"There were six of us altogether, patrolling that part of the beach, so we consulted together, and thought it best that four should remain behind and keep the hut in sight, and that I and my comrade should come at once to report what we had seen."

"You saw nothing of the tall stranger?"

"Nothing, citizen. We met half a dozen men just now,

who have been patrolling this road for several hours and they have seen no stranger either."

"Yet he is on ahead somewhere, in a cart or something else. There is not a moment to lose. How far is that hut from here?"

"About a couple of leagues, citizen."

"Can you find it again – at once – without hesitation?"

"I am sure of it, citizen."

"The footpath, to the edge of the cliff? Even in the dark?"

"It is not a dark night, citizen, and I know I can find my way," repeated the soldier, firmly.

"Fall in behind. Let your comrade take both your horses back to Calais. You won't want them. Keep beside the cart, and direct this old man to drive straight ahead; then stop him, within a quarter of a league of the footpath; see that he takes the most direct road."

While Chauvelin spoke, Desgas and his men were fast approaching, and Marguerite could hear their footsteps within a hundred yards behind her now.

It was unsafe to stay where she was. She heard the soldier giving a few brief directions to the old man, then she retired quickly to the edge of the road, and hid behind some low shrubs, while Desgas and his men came up.

All fell in noiselessly behind the cart, and slowly they all started down the dark road. Marguerite waited for several minutes, then she, too, in the darkness, which suddenly seemed to have become more intense, crept noiselessly along.

CHAPTER 28

The Père Blanchard's Hut

As in a dream, Marguerite followed on. The web was drawing more and more tightly every moment around her beloved husband. She had little hope now of saving him and only prayed that she would see him once again to tell him how she loved him and how sorry she was for having wronged and misunderstood him and how she had suffered for him.

The distant roar of the waves now made her shudder; the occasional dismal cry of an owl, or a seagull, filled her with horror. She thought of the ravenous beasts in human form who lay in wait for their prey to satisfy their own appetite of hate.

Marguerite was not afraid of the darkness. She only feared that man, on ahead, who was sitting at the bottom of a rough wooden cart, nursing thoughts of vengeance which would have made the very demons in hell chuckle with delight.

Her feet were sore. Her knees shook under her because she was so tired. She had not had a rest for three nights;

119

now, she had walked on a slippery road for nearly two hours, but she was steadfast. She would see her husband, tell him all, and, if he was ready to forgive the crime which she had committed in her blind ignorance, she would yet have the happiness of dying by his side.

Presently she realized that the cart had stopped and that Chauvelin had got out and was giving some orders to his men. Then she saw them all turn off sharply to the right of the road, apparently on to the footpath which led to the cliffs. The old man had remained on the road with his horse and cart. After a minute or two, one of the soldiers came back, put a gag on the old man and made him follow the party. Evidently Chauvelin feared he might see the tall stranger first and warn him.

When they were all out of sight, Marguerite also turned to the right. She crawled on her hands and knees through rough, low shrubs, trying to make as little noise as possible as she went along, tearing her face and hands against the dry twigs and keeping as quiet as she could. Fortunately the footpath was bordered by a low, rough hedge behind which was a dry ditch, filled with coarse grass. In this Marguerite managed to find shelter; she was quite hidden from view, yet she managed to get within three yards of where Chauvelin stood giving further orders to his men, at a point where the path began to descend the cliff.

Chauvelin was instructing his men not to enter the hut unless the tall stranger was in there with the fugitives and, if he was, to make sure they took him alive. Then the party started off again.

For the moment Marguerite could do nothing but follow the soldiers and Chauvelin. She feared to lose her way, or she would have rushed forward and found that wooden hut, and perhaps been in time to warn the fugitives and their brave deliverer.

Suddenly she cowered down within the shadow of the hedge. The moon, which had proved a friend to her by

120

remaining hidden behind a bank of clouds, now emerged in all the glory of an early autumn night, and in a moment flooded the weird and lonely landscape with a rush of brilliant light. There, not two hundred metres ahead, was the edge of the cliff, stretching far away to free and happy England; the sea rolled on smoothly and peaceably. Marguerite's gaze rested for an instant on the brilliant, silvery waters, and, as she gazed, she saw that not three miles away, with white sails set, a graceful schooner lay in wait.

She felt sure it must be the *Day Dream*, Percy's favourite yacht, with old Briggs, that prince of skippers, and her crew of British sailors aboard. The sight of the schooner filled Marguerite with joy and hope. The moon was out and she decided to find her way down to the hut, rouse the people in it and warn them at any rate to sell their lives dearly, rather than let them be caught like so many rats in a hole.

Marguerite stumbled on behind the hedge in the low, thick grass of the ditch. She must have run on very fast, for she could now hear Chauvelin and Desgas behind her and she had reached the edge of the cliff.

Marguerite peered cautiously down and saw at some little distance on her left, and about midway down the cliffs, a rough wooden hut, through the walls of which a tiny red light glimmered like a beacon. Without hesitation she began the steep descent, creeping from rock to rock, caring nothing for the enemy behind or for the soldiers, who evidently had all taken cover, since the tall Englishman had not yet appeared.

On she pressed, forgetting the deadly foe on her track, running, stumbling, footsore, half-dazed, but still on. When, suddenly, a crevice, or stone, or slippery bit of rock, threw her violently to the ground, she struggled again to her feet, and went on, thinking only of those she had come to warn.

But now Marguerite realized that other steps, quicker than her own, were already close at her heels. The next instant a hand dragged at her skirt, and she was down on her knees again, while something was wound round her mouth to prevent her uttering a scream.

Bewildered, half frantic with the bitterness of disappointment, she looked round her helplessly, and, bending down quite close to her, she saw through the mist, which seemed to gather round her, a pair of keen malicious eyes, which appeared to her feverish brain to have a weird, ghostly green light in them.

She lay in the shadow of a great boulder; Chauvelin could not see her features, but he passed his thin, white fingers over her face.

"A woman," he whispered, "by all the saints in the calendar."

"We cannot let her loose, that's certain," he muttered to himself. "I wonder . . ."

Suddenly he paused, and after a few seconds of deadly silence, he gave forth a long, low, curious chuckle, while once again Marguerite felt, with a horrible shudder, his thin fingers wandering over her face.

"Dear me, dear me," he whispered, "this is indeed a charming surprise," and Marguerite felt her limp hand raised to Chauvelin's thin, mocking lips.

Chauvelin must have given some directions which she was too dazed to hear, for she felt herself lifted from her feet; the bandage round her mouth was made more secure and a pair of strong arms carried her towards that tiny, red light, on ahead, which she had looked upon as a beacon and the last faint glimmer of hope.

CHAPTER 29

Trapped

Marguerite did not know how long she was carried along in this state; she had lost all notion of time and space, and for a short time she lost consciousness.

When she came to, she realized that the end of the journey had been reached for she could hear rapid questions and answers spoken in a whisper quite close to her.

"There are four men in there, citizen; they are sitting by the fire, and seem to be waiting quietly."

"The hour?"

"Nearly two o'clock."

"The tide?"

"Coming in quickly."

"The schooner?"

"Obviously an English one, lying some three kilometres out, but we cannot see her boat."

"Have the men taken cover?"

"Yes, citizen."

"They will not blunder?"

"They will not stir until the tall Englishman comes, then they will surround and overpower the five men."

"Right. And the lady?"

"Still dazed, I fancy. She's close beside you, citizen."

"And the old man?"

"He's gagged, and his legs strapped together. He cannot move or scream."

"Good. Then have your gun ready, in case you want it. Get close to the hut and leave me to look after the lady."

Desgas evidently obeyed, for Marguerite heard him creeping away along the stony cliff, then she felt that a pair of warm, thin, talonlike hands took hold of both her own, and held them in a grip of steel.

"Before the handkerchief is removed from that pretty mouth, fair lady," whispered Chauvelin, "I think it right to tell you that I have guessed your intentions. You have come here, to warn not only the fugitives, but your brother Armand and the Scarlet Pimpernel himself. If you do so, my soldiers will shoot them all here before your eyes."

Marguerite listened with horror. Though dazed with pain, she realized that Chauvelin was again putting before her the terrible "either – or."

This time it meant that she should keep still and allow her adored husband to walk unknowingly to his death or that she should, by trying to give him a word of warning, actually give the signal for her own brother's death, and that of those other unsuspecting men.

Chauvelin removed the handkerchief from her mouth. She certainly did not scream: at that moment she had not strength to do anything but barely hold herself upright, and to force herself to think. What could she do but sit there and wait! The hours dragged on and still it was not dawn: the sea continued its incessant mournful murmur, the autumnal breeze sighed gently in the night: the lonely beach was silent, even as the grave.

Suddenly from somewhere, not very far away, a cheerful strong voice was heard singing "God Save the King".

CHAPTER 30

The Schooner

The voice came nearer and nearer and Marguerite distinctly heard the click of Desgas' gun close to her. With a wild shriek she sprang to her feet, and darted round the rock, against which she had been cowering: she saw the little red gleam through the chinks of the hut; she ran up to it and fell against its wooden walls which she began to hammer with clenched fists in a frenzy, while she shouted –

"Armand! Armand! For God's sake, fire! Your leader is coming! He is betrayed! Armand! Armand! Fire, in heaven's name!"

She was seized and thrown to the ground. She lay there moaning, bruised, not caring, but still half sobbing, half shrieking –

"Percy, my husband, for God's sake fly! Armand! Armand! Why don't you fire?"

"One of you stop that woman screaming," hissed Chauvelin, who could hardly refrain from striking her.

Something was thrown over her face; she could not breathe, and she was silent.

The bold singer, too, had become silent. The men had sprung to their feet; there was no need for further silence on their part. Chauvelin gave the command, with a muttered oath –

"Into it, my men, and let no one escape from that hut alive!"

The moon had once more emerged from between the clouds: the darkness on the cliffs had gone, giving place once more to brilliant, silvery light. Some of the soldiers had rushed to the rough, wooden door of the hut, while one of them kept guard over Marguerite.

The door was partly open; one of the soldiers pushed it a little, but within all was darkness, the charcoal fire only lighting with a dim, red light the farthest corner of the hut. The soldiers paused automatically at the door, like machines, waiting for further orders.

Filled with anxiety, Chauvelin, too, went to the door of the hut and asked the men why they were waiting.

"I think, citizen, there is no one there now," replied one of the men.

"You have not let those four men go?" thundered Chauvelin threateningly, as he looked inside the hut. "I ordered you to let no man escape alive! Quick, after them, all of you! Quick, in every direction!"

The men, obedient as machines, rushed down the rocky slope towards the beach as fast as their feet could carry them.

"You and your men will pay with your lives for this blunder, citizen sergeant," said Chauvelin viciously to the soldier who had been in charge of the men; "and you too, Citizen Desgas," he added, "for disobeying my orders."

"You ordered us to wait, citizen, until the tall Englishman arrived and joined the four men in the hut. No one came," said the sergeant sullenly.

"But I ordered you just now, when the woman screamed, to rush in and let no one escape."

"They were gone by then," said the sergeant. "I heard the men creep out of the hut, not many minutes after we took cover and long before the woman screamed," he added, as Chauvelin seemed still quite speechless with rage.

"Hark!" said Desgas suddenly.

In the distance the sound of repeated firing was heard.

The firing stopped. All three men listened attentively. In the far, very far distance, could be heard faintly echoing and already dying away, the quick, sharp splash of half a

126

dozen oars. Chauvelin took out his handkerchief and wiped the perspiration from his forehead.

"The schooner's boat!" was all he gasped.

Evidently Armand St Just and his three companions had managed to creep along the side of the cliffs, while the soldiers had, with blind obedience, and in fear of their lives, obeyed Chauvelin's orders – to wait for the tall Englishman, who was the important capture.

The fugitives must have reached one of the creeks which jut far out to sea on this coast at intervals; behind this, the boat of the *Day Dream* would have been on the lookout for them; and they were by now safely on board the British schooner.

As if to confirm this, the dull boom of a gun was heard from out at sea.

"The schooner, citizen," said Desgas, quietly; "she's off."

There remained the bold singer. Where had he got to? He could not have covered that mile on a rocky cliff in the space of two minutes; and only two minutes had passed between his song, Marguerite's scream and the sound of the boat's oars away at sea. He must have remained behind, and perhaps was even now hiding somewhere about the cliffs; the patrols were still about; he would be sighted no doubt. Chauvelin felt hopeful once again.

"Bring the light in here," he commanded, as he entered the hut.

The sergeant brought his lantern, and together the two men explored it. With a rapid glance Chauvelin noted its contents: the cauldron placed close under a hole in the wall, containing the last few dying embers of burned charcoal, a couple of stools, overturned as if in the haste of a sudden departure, then the fisherman's tools and his nets lying in one corner, and beside them, something small and white.

"Pick that up," said Chauvelin to the sergeant, pointing to this white scrap, "and bring it to me."

It was a crumpled piece of paper, evidently forgotten

127

by the fugitives in their hurry to get away. The sergeant picked the paper up and handed it respectfully to Chauvelin.

"Read it, Sergeant."

"It is hard to read, citizen, a fearful scrawl."

The sergeant, by the light of his lantern, began deciphering the few hastily scrawled words.

"I cannot reach you without risking your lives. When you receive this, wait two minutes, then creep out of the hut one by one, turn to your left sharply, and creep cautiously down the cliff; keep to the left all the time, till you reach the first rock, which you see jutting far out to sea – behind it in the creek the boat is on the lookout for you – give a long, sharp whistle – she will come up – get into her – my men will row you to the schooner, and from there to England and safety – once on board the Day Dream send the boat back for me, tell my men that I shall be at the creek which is in a direct line opposite the Chat Gris near Calais. They know it. I shall be there as soon as possible – they must wait for me at a safe distance out at sea – till they hear the usual signal. Do not delay – and obey these instructions.

"Then there is the signature, citizen," added the sergeant, as he handed back the paper to Chauvelin.

One sentence stood out for Chauvelin –

"I shall be at the creek which is in a direct line opposite the Chat Gris near Calais": he might yet get his man.

"Which of you knows this coast well?" he shouted to the soldiers, who now one by one had all returned and were assembled once more around the hut.

"I do, citizen," said one of them. "I was born in Calais, and know every stone of these cliffs."

"Is there a creek in a direct line from the Chat Gris?"

"There is, citizen, I know it well."

"The Englishman is hoping to reach that creek. There is a chance to get him yet. A thousand francs to each man who gets to that creek before the long-legged Englishman."

128

"I know a short cut across the cliffs," said the soldier, and with an enthusiastic shout he rushed forward, followed closely by his comrades.

Two soldiers were holding Marguerite pinioned to the ground, though she, poor soul, was not making the faintest struggle, for she had fainted. The sight aroused no pity in Chauvelin.

"It is no use mounting guard over a woman who is half dead," he said spitefully to the soldiers, "when you have allowed five men who were very much alive to escape."

Obediently the soldiers rose to their feet.

"You'd better try and find that footpath again for me, and that broken-down cart we left on the road."

Then suddenly a bright idea seemed to strike him.

"That reminds me. Where is that stupid old man?"

"Close by here, citizen," said Desgas; "I gagged him and tied his legs together as you commanded, in case he should prove a nuisance."

From nearby, a plaintive moan was heard. Chauvelin followed his secretary, who led the way to the other side of the hut where the poor old driver of the cart lay, his mouth gagged and his legs tied together. He looked exhausted and terrified.

The rope which was originally round his shoulders and arms had evidently given way, for it lay in a tangle about his body, but he did not seem aware of this, for he had not made the slightest attempt to move from the place where Desgas had left him.

"Bring him over here," commanded Chauvelin. He was in a vicious mood, but since he could not very well punish the soldiers for simply obeying orders, he decided to vent his rage on the unfortunate old man.

"Do you remember our bargain?" he said as Desgas undid the gag.

"Yes, citizen," replied the old man, trembling.

"It was agreed between us that if we overtook my friend

129

the tall stranger before we reached this place, you were to be well rewarded."

A low moan came from the old man who was shaking all over.

"But," said Chauvelin, "if you deceived me, you were to have a sound beating to teach you not to tell lies and make promises you could not keep."

Another moan.

"Here," said Chauvelin, to the two soldiers, "take the buckle-ends of your belts to this old man, but do not kill him."

He did not wait to see his orders carried out. He knew the soldiers would obey him without thought as usual.

"When that old fool has had his punishment," he said to Desgas, "the men can guide us as far as the cart, and one of them can drive us back in it to Calais The old man and the woman can look after each other," he added roughly, "until we can send someone for them in the morning. They can't run away very far in their present condition, and we cannot be troubled with them just now."

Chauvelin turned and took a last look at the lonely bit of coast, where stood the hut, now bathed in moonlight. He had lost the battle here, but still hoped to win the final one against his old enemy, the Scarlet Pimpernel.

Against a rock, on a hard bed of stone lay the unconscious figure of Marguerite Blakeney while some few paces further on, the wretched old man was receiving on his broad back the blows from the soldiers's belts. His cries were fit to make the dead rise from their graves.

"That will do," commanded Chauvelin, "we don't want to kill him."

The old man was lying on the ground and appeared to have fainted.

"Leave him there," said Chauvelin, "and lead the way now quickly to the cart. I'll follow."

He walked up to where Marguerite lay and looked down

into her face. She had evidently recovered consciousness for she was struggling to raise herself and her large blue eyes were observing with pity and horror the sufferings of the old man.

Chauvelin kissed her hand with mock gallantry.

"I must leave you, fair lady," he said, "but at dawn I will send an escort for you. In the meantime our friend over there, though a trifle the worse for wear, will look after you. You will find him devoted though rather slow."

Marguerite turned her head away. As she returned to consciousness, she had only one thought – "What had become of Percy? What of Armand?"

"Farewell, Madame," said Chauvelin sarcastically, "we shall meet perhaps at the Prince of Wales' garden party!"

He bowed and disappeared down the path in the wake of the soldiers, followed by his loyal secretary, Citizen Desgas.

CHAPTER 31

The Escape

Marguerite lay there for some time. She was so exhausted that she wished she could lie there forever. All was solitary and silent, as in a dream. Even the last faint echo of the distant cart had long ago died away, afar.

Suddenly a sound, the strangest perhaps, that these lonely cliffs of France had ever heard, broke the silence.

It was the sound of a good, solid, British "Damn!"

The seagulls in their nests awoke and looked round in astonishment; a distant and solitary owl set up a midnight hoot, the tall cliffs frowned down majestically on the disturbance.

Marguerite did not trust her ears, but the voice came again –

"Odd's life. But I wish those demmed fellows had not hit quite so hard."

This time there was no mistake about it. Only one person could have uttered those words, in sleepy, drawly, affected tones.

"Zounds," said the voice, "but I'm as weak as a rat."

In a moment Marguerite was on her feet. She looked round her eagerly at the tall cliffs, the lonely hut, the great stretch of rocky beach. Somewhere there above or below her, behind a boulder or inside a crevice, but still hidden from her longing, feverish eyes, must be the owner of that voice, which once used to irritate her, but now would make her the happiest woman in Europe, if only she could find it.

"Percy! Percy!" she called. "I am here. Come to me."

"It's all very well calling me, m'dear, but I cannot come to you. Those demmed frog-eaters have trussed me like a goose on a spit, and I am as weak as a mouse. I cannot get away."

And still Marguerite did not understand. Where could the voice be coming from? There was no one within sight . . . except by that rock. Great God! . . . the old man! . . . was she mad or dreaming?

His back was against the pale moonlight, he was half-crouching, trying vainly to raise himself with his arms tightly bound. Marguerite ran up to him, took his head in both her hands . . . and looked straight into a pair of blue eyes, good-natured, even a trifle amused – shining out of the pathetic, dirty face of the old man.

"Percy . . . Percy . . . my husband," she gasped. "Thank God. Thank God."

"We will both do that, m'dear," he rejoined good-humouredly, "if you can release me from these demmed ropes."

She had no knife, her fingers were numb and weak, but she worked away with her teeth, while great welcome tears poured from her eyes onto those poor, pinioned hands.

It was very obvious that her husband was exhausted from the pain, and when at last the rope gave way, he fell in a heap against the rock.

133

Marguerite looked helplessly round her.

"Oh! for a drop of water on this awful beach," she cried in agony, seeing he was ready to faint again.

"Personally I should prefer a drop of good French brandy. If you'll dive in the pocket of this dirty old coat, you'll find my flask. I am demmed if I can move."

When he had drunk some brandy, he forced Marguerite to do the same.

"That's better, eh, little woman?" he said with a sigh of satisfaction. "Heigh-ho, but this is a queer rig-up for Sir Percy Blakeney to be found in by his lady, and no mistake. Begad!" he added, passing his hand over his chin, "I haven't been shaved for nearly twenty hours: I must look a disgusting object. As for this hair . . ."

And laughingly he took off a wig of matted dirty locks, and stretched out his long limbs, which were cramped from many hours' stooping. Then he bent forward and looked long and searchingly into his wife's blue eyes.

"Percy," she whispered, "if you only knew . . ."

"I do know, dear . . . everything," he said gently.

"And can you ever forgive?"

"I have nothing to forgive, sweetheart; your bravery and devotion, which, alas I so little deserve, more than make up for that unfortunate episode at the ball."

"Then you knew," she whispered, "all the time?"

"Yes," he replied tenderly, "I knew all the time. But had I known what a noble heart yours was, I should have trusted you, as you deserved to be trusted, and you would not have had to undergo the terrible sufferings of the past few hours, in order to run after a husband who has done so much that needs forgiveness."

They were sitting side by side, leaning up against a rock, and he had rested his aching head on her shoulder. She thought she must be the happiest woman in Europe.

"It is a case of the blind leading the lame, sweetheart, is it not?" he said with his good-natured smile. "Odd's life.

But I do not know which are the more sore, my shoulders or your little feet."

He bent forward to kiss them, for they peeped out through her torn stockings, and were a pathetic witness to her endurance and devotion.

"But what of Armand?" she said, with sudden terror and remorse, for it was on his account that she had so deeply sinned.

"Armand is safe, as I promised he would be. He is on board the *Day Dream* with de Tournay and the others."

"But I cannot see how you managed it."

"It is simple enough, m'dear. When I found that that brute Chauvelin meant to stick to me like a leech, I thought the best thing I could do was to take him along with me. I had to get to Armand and the others somehow, and all the roads were patrolled, and everyone was on the lookout for me. I knew that when I slipped through Chauvelin's fingers at the Chat Gris, that he would lie in wait for me here, whichever way I took. I wanted to keep an eye on him and his doings, and a British head is as good as a French one any day."

Indeed it had proved infinitely better, and Marguerite listened full of wonder and joy as he told of the daring manner in which he had snatched the fugitives away, right from under Chauvelin's very nose.

"Dressed as a shabby old man," he said, smiling, "I knew I should not be recognized. I had met Reuben in Calais earlier in the evening. For a few gold pieces he supplied me with this rig-out – the wig was a masterpiece – and he undertook to keep out of sight while I went off with his horse and cart."

"And then what happened?" asked Marguerite breathlessly.

"Then, as you now know, Chauvelin hired me to take him and Desgas to the Père Blanchard's hut. At first I determined to leave everything to chance, but when I heard Chauvelin giving his orders to the soldiers, I thought that Fate was on my side. I reckoned on the blind obedience of the soldiers.

135

Chauvelin had ordered them not to move until the tall Englishman came.

"Desgas had put me down on the ground quite close to the hut. They had tied me up and gagged me, because they trusted nobody and they feared I might give the alarm. Anyhow I was only an unimportant old man who had served his purpose and they took no further notice of me.

"When all was quiet, I managed to free my hands from the ropes with which the brutes had trussed me; I always carry pencil and paper with me wherever I go, and hastily scrawled a few important instructions on a scrap of paper; then I looked about me. I crawled up to the hut, under the very noses of the soldiers, who lay under cover without moving just as Chauvelin had ordered them to do, then I dropped my little note into the hut, through a chink in the wall, and waited. I waited for nearly half an hour. When I knew the fugitives were safe, I gave the signal which caused so much stir."

And that was the whole story of his daring plan.

He put his arm round his wife and they laughed together, but suddenly the light of joy died out of her eyes: she had heard a stealthy footfall overhead, and a stone had rolled down from the top of the cliffs right down to the beach below.

"What's that?" she whispered in horror and alarm.

"Only our friend Ffoulkes," said Sir Percy. "Fortunately I met him not far from the Chat Gris, before I had that interesting supper party with my friend Chauvelin, with whom I have a few scores to settle. I told Ffoulkes of a very long, very roundabout road, almost certainly unknown to most of the soldiers, which would bring him here just about the time we were ready for him."

Marguerite felt a pang; she had forgotten all about her loyal friend!

In the meantime Sir Andrew had worked his way down

the cliffs and was astonished to find an old ragged man and a woman in torn clothing leaning against a rock.

"Welcome, my friend," said Sir Percy, calmly, "I have not yet had time to ask you what you were doing in France when I ordered you to remain in London? Disobedience? Wait until my shoulders are less sore and see the punishment you will get!"

"Faith and I'll bear it," said Sir Andrew, with a merry laugh, "seeing that you are alive to give it. Would you have me allow Lady Blakeney to do the journey alone? But, in the name of heaven, man, where did you get those fusty old clothes?"

"Lud! They are a bit quaint, ain't they?" laughed Sir Percy. "But to look to our plans, Ffoulkes, now that you are here, we must lose no more time: that brute Chauvelin may send someone to look after us."

"But how can we escape?" asked Marguerite, alarmed. "The roads are full of soldiers between here and Calais and we have just heard them firing from the beach."

"We are not going back to Calais, sweetheart, and we are not going down to the beach below here," he said, "but to just the other side of Gris Nez, not half a league from here. The boat of the *Day Dream* will meet us there."

"The boat of the *Day Dream?*"

"Yes. I should have told you before that when I slipped that note into the hut, I added another for Armand which I directed him to leave behind.

"That note was found by one of Chauvelin's men, and it sent his master running full tilt after me to the Chat Gris. The first note contained my real instructions to old Briggs. He had my orders to go farther out to sea, and then towards the west. When he is well out of sight of Calais, he will send the boat to a little creek which he and I know of just beyond Gris-Nez. The men will look out for me – we have arranged a signal, and we will all be safely on board, while Chauvelin and his men solemnly sit and watch the creek opposite the Chat Gris."

"The other side of Gris-Nez? But I cannot walk, Percy."

"I will carry you, dear," he said simply; "the blind leading the lame, you know."

Sir Andrew wanted to help him, but Sir Percy would not entrust his beloved to any arms but his own.

"I will rest when you and she are safely on board the *Day Dream*," he said, "and I can hand you back safely to Mademoiselle Suzanne."

And his arms, still vigorous in spite of fatigue and suffering, closed round Marguerite's poor, weary body, and lifted her as gently as if she had been a feather.

Then, as Sir Andrew walked a little apart, there were many things whispered which even the autumn breeze did not catch, for it had gone to rest.

The many-hued light of dawn was breaking in the east, when at last they reached the creek beyond Gris-Nez. The boat lay there, waiting. In answer to a signal from Sir Percy she drew near, and two sturdy British sailors had the honour of carrying my lady into the boat.

Half an hour later, they were on board the *Day Dream*, where Armand St Just and the other fugitives were eagerly awaiting them. Nobody was surprised to see their brave rescuer in disguise, and by the time they reached England he had changed into the sumptuous clothes he liked so much.

The difficulty was to find a pair of shoes for Marguerite, but a very young, very small cadet offered his best pair and was happy when they were accepted.

The rest is silence – silence and joy for those who had endured so much suffering, yet found at last a great and lasting happiness.

But it is on record that, at the brilliant wedding of Sir Andrew Ffoulkes, Baronet, with Mademoiselle Suzanne de Tournay de Basserive, a function attended by H.R.H. the Prince of Wales and all of fashionable society, the most beautiful woman there, apart from the bride, was Lady Blakeney, and the best-dressed man was her husband, Sir Percy.

It is also a fact that Monsieur Chauvelin, the official representative of the French Republican Government, was not present at that or any other social function in London, after that memorable evening at Lord Grenville's ball.

Armada
Gift Classics

An attractive collection of beautifully illustrated stories, including some of the finest and most enjoyable children's stories ever written.

Some of the older, longer titles have been skilfully edited and abridged.

ARMADA

All these books are available at your local bookshop or newsagent, or can be ordered from the publisher. To order direct from the publishers just tick the titles you want and fill in the form below:

Name _____

Address _____

_____

Send to: Collins Childrens Cash Sales
          PO Box 11
          Falmouth
          Cornwall
          TR10 9EN

Please enclose a cheque or postal order or debit my Visa/Access –

Credit card no:

Expiry date:

Signature:

– to the value of the cover price plus:

UK: 60p for the first book, 25p for the second book, plus 15p per copy for each additional book ordered to a maximum charge of £1.90.

BFPO: 60p for the first book, 25p for the second book plus 15p per copy for the next 7 books, thereafter 9p per book.

Overseas and Eire: £1.25 for the first book, 75p for the second book. Thereafter 28p per book.

ARMADA